Eep!

Joke van Leeuwen

Eep!

Joke van Leeuwen

Translated by Bill Nagelkerke

GECKO PRESS

First American edition published in 2012 by Gecko Press USA,
an imprint of Gecko Press Ltd.

A catalog record for this book is available from the US Library of Congress.

Distributed in the United States and Canada by
Lerner Publishing Group, Inc.
241 First Avenue North
Minneapolis, MN 55401 USA
www.lernerbooks.com

This edition first published in 2012 by Gecko Press
PO Box 9335, Marion Square, Wellington 6141, New Zealand
info@geckopress.com

Translated by Bill Nagelkerke
Cover design by Spencer Levine, Wellington, New Zealand
Typeset by Archetype, Wellington, New Zealand
Printed by Everbest, China

Publication of *Eep!* was aided by a subsidy from the Foundation for
the Production and Translation of Dutch Literature and the
Mondriaan Foundation.

ISBN hardback: 978-1-877579-07-3

For more curiously good books, visit www.geckopress.com

TAKE THREE LINES.

CURVE THEM A LITTLE.

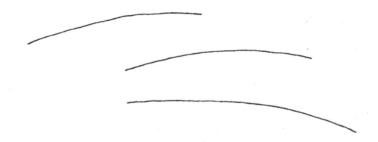

JOIN THEM TOGETHER.

AND HERE IS THE LANDSCAPE
IN WHICH THIS STORY BEGINS.

IMAGINE THE SUN SHINING ABOVE IT ALL,
EVEN THOUGH IT DOESN'T FIT ONTO THE PAGE.
BUSHES AND TREES HAVE TO BE ADDED.

AS WELL AS PATHS.

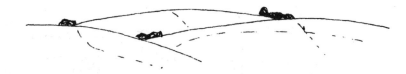

PEOPLE SOMETIMES USE THE PATHS AND SO
DO BEETLES AND SNAILS. BEETLES AND SNAILS
DON'T KNOW THEY'RE WALKING ON THEM.
PEOPLE DO. LIKE THE MAN IN THE DISTANCE.
HE'S LOOKING AT THE BIRDS. AND HE KNOWS IT.

1

Warren liked birds. He thought birdwatching was one of the best things you could do in life. Much better than looking at paintings or staring at television.

Every day Warren wandered through the countryside near his house. The landscape looked like three curved lines, with bushes and trees and pathways and the sun above it all, as long as it was a nice summer.

Warren always carried a pair of binoculars. Birds don't like it when you get too close to them. And he had a bird book. Birds from miles around were listed in that book with their names, their colors and their faces.

(Do birds really have faces? People and animals have a lot in common. Sometimes they even look alike.)

Whenever Warren saw a bird, he checked that all its details matched those in his bird book. When everything matched, he got a warm feeling inside, somewhere around his middle. He wished there was a book like that about the whole world, where everything matched up.

One day, when Warren was wandering through the country-side, he looked under a bush. He didn't usually do that. Usually he only looked up at the sky or into trees, but not under bushes. However, that day that's what he did. He had the sudden impression he'd seen a bird lying there, a big bird of prey. As it turned out, it was something quite different, something not mentioned in his bird book. Something with wings, however, and with legs and feet. But those legs and feet looked a lot like human legs and feet. Especially the feet, with their small toes and tiny toenails and smidgens of dirt underneath the toenails on the toes on the feet on the legs.

What Warren saw lying there looked very much like a human child, except it had feathers instead of clothes. And where the arms should have been, there were wings. Real ones.

Just for a second, Warren thought an angel had fallen from the sky. But of course he knew this wasn't an angel because angels had arms. Angels had wings on their backs and arms where arms were supposed to be. At least, that's what people had always believed about angels.

But no. This was a bird in the shape of a little girl. Or a little girl in the shape of a bird. Or something in between.

She was asleep. Perhaps she's been abandoned, thought Warren. That was something people did in the old days, when they didn't have enough money or if their child didn't fit in. They would lay the child down somewhere, hoping it would be found. In front of a door, perhaps, or in a window box. Of course, you sometimes saw a grown person lying in a doorway or in a flowerbed, but that was a different matter entirely. No one imagined they'd been left there for someone else to find.

Anyway, birds didn't abandon their babies.

Warren lifted the creature up and nestled it in his arms. Two eyes opened briefly and closed again. Warren looked up and down the track, left, right, and left again.

He didn't see anybody. Just two beetles.

"Hey!" he called out. "Does this belong to anyone?"

No one answered. There was only the sound of a familiar bird screeching. And that bird was listed in his book.

Warren shouted, "Listen, I'm taking this with me. I'm taking it!" And he took the bird-child home, arranging his arms so they resembled a nest. The binoculars dangled down his back.

This doesn't make sense, he kept telling himself. It's not possible.

But he knew he was carrying the proof in his arms.

2

Warren lived with his wife Tina in a small house behind the hills. It was a house full of gaps. If you were lying in bed when soup was being made, you'd smell it right away. Of course, soup wasn't usually being made then. Who wants soup when they're lying in bed?

Warren came in with his arms full. At first Tina didn't notice a thing because she was busy watching television. People were talking to each other about horrible illnesses.

About shocking spots.

Awful wrinkles.

Horrendous headaches.

Hearing all that, Tina forgot she was perfectly healthy.

"Look at this," said Warren.

Tina turned round.

"What have you got there?" she asked.

"Something I found," said Warren.

Tina stared at the bundle in Warren's arms. Carefully, she touched it.

"This doesn't make any sense," she said. "It's got wings."

"Yes," agreed Warren. "And legs."

"Was it just lying somewhere?"

"Yes, it was," said Warren. "There was no note with it. I even called out, asking if it belonged to someone."

Tina took the abandoned child in her arms. She felt its wings to see if they really were attached.

"She's alive," she said.

"Yes," said Warren, "so I guess that means she really exists."

"I'd like to keep her," said Tina. She stroked the sleeping head. "Although shouldn't we hand her in to the police? That's what you do with lost children."

"With a lost child, yes," said Warren, "but not with a bird."

"Surely she can't be in your bird book?"

"No. This is a rare kind of bird. It might be the only one. Although I think they existed long ago."

"She seems more like a person than a bird," said Tina.

"Take a good look," said Warren. "It has two little feet. They look like human feet, but a bird has feet as well. It has a small head, very like a human head, but a bird has a head, too. And it has two wings. All birds have those. People don't. So I'd say it's more a bird than a person."

"You can pretend she's a bird if you want to," said Tina, "but she's a child as far as I'm concerned. And she needs some milk and pieces of fruit."

"What about birdseed? Try some of that, too."

The foundling suddenly opened her eyes. And her mouth. Her face reddened with effort.

She squeezed out a sound. "Eep!"

But that was all.

3

In the shed behind the house, Tina found an old basket that resembled both a bed and a nest. She dressed the birdlike girl in one of Warren's undershirts and laid her in the basket with a pillowcase for a sheet.

Warren fetched two kitchen chairs. He and Tina sat side by side. Together they gazed down into the basket. It takes time to get used to something new.

"No one must know," said Tina. "She's very rare, and other people often want what's rare. We'll have to hide her wings."

"Yes," agreed Warren. "We'll have to hide her wings."

Together they went on looking, in silence.

Eventually Warren said, "She'll have to have a name. Birds always have names, even if not many people know what they are."

"She can't have a bird's name," said Tina. "They're all hard-to-learn Latin names. Far too heavy to carry around."

"That's not true," said Warren. "Birds can have much easier names as well. Like chaffinch or sparrow or blackbird or fantail or magpie or bellbird or dotterel or quail or grebe or swallow or linnet."

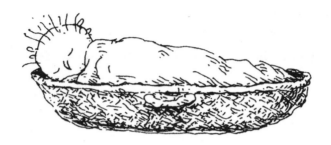

"I'd go dotty if I was called Dotterel," said Tina. "I'd want something nicer than that."

"The great thing is," said Warren, "we can make up a name for our foundling because *we* found her. I'm sure this sort of bird doesn't have a name already. There's no mention of it in my book. We can give her our own name. You're allowed to do that when you find a new species. It's like someone discovering a disease and naming it after himself."

"Who'd want a disease named after them? I wouldn't! Anyway, why are you talking about diseases? Just when something nice happens, you start going on about diseases."

They tried out a whole lot of names. They tried them out while looking into the basket to see how well they suited.

Baby Bird, they said, and Tiny Flyer and Bicycle Bell ("What's *that* supposed to mean?" "I was just trying it out.").

They tried Little Peep and Flutter and Flapper and Cheep and Juliana.

But at long last they called her Birdy. And they were both happy with that.

("Or is Little Peep better?")

("No, no.")

("Okay then.")

4

Warren and Tina bought clothes for Birdy. They fitted her lower half well but not her top half. Tina cut big holes in the top layers for Birdy's wings to poke through. She also made a wide jacket cape, which looked rather like a tent awning. It swallowed Birdy's wings. No one could see that she had them.

Tina also bought a nice stroller with pictures of puffy white clouds. She lay Birdy inside. Now she looked exactly like a normal child, *their* child. Birdy gazed up at the sky and said, "Eep! Eep!"

Tina and Warren were very proud that she could say "eep."

"It's as if she's learnt a word already," said Tina.

No one could be allowed to find out about the wings. Because then people would gossip. And everyone would want to come and steal a look. They might well believe that Birdy *was* an angel. After all, no one knew terribly much about angels. They might ask the angel to fix things up for them, like getting rid of shocking spots or awful wrinkles or horrendous headaches. And that would cause far too many problems.

Occasionally someone looked into the stroller. A large head would blot out the sky.

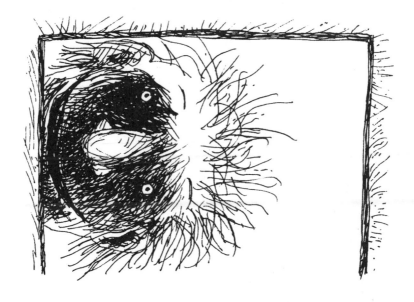

Sometimes people asked, "Is she yours?"

And Warren would answer, "She's on loan to us."

Then they'd want to know where you could borrow a child. Some people seemed to think it would be very handy to be able to choose a child and return it if you changed your mind.

"She comes from far away," Tina told anybody who asked. "You have to be in the know to know about such things."

Then she would take a quick peek into the stroller.

You could see two little bumps. Only bumps, but anything at all could be under them.

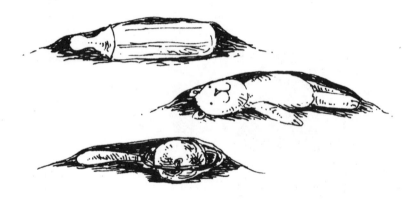

Who would guess, on an ordinary street, in summer, that they were hidden wings?

5

Birdy grew quickly. She changed as much in a week as any other child would in a year. The only thing was, she stayed smaller and lighter than other children.

Soon Birdy was climbing out of her basket and trying to walk. Learning to walk isn't easy. All creatures find the first steps the hardest.

But Birdy found it easy. If she was about to topple over, she would flutter her wings a little and right herself. Weighing next to nothing gave her a big advantage.

She improved by leaps and bounds, each leap and each bound lasting a little longer. Soon she could flap a few feet up, fluttering from one wall to the other.

Once again, Warren and Tina sat on their kitchen chairs and watched from the sideline.

"See how handy flying is?" said Tina. "I never realized that before. Have you ever thought: if only I could fly?"

"No, never," said Warren. "I've never thought I was missing out on anything, but it must be a great thing, being able to fly. Being so *light*. It's a shame we can't."

"I sometimes fly inside my head," said Tina, "but we could never actually do it on the outside."

They gave it a try though because you never knew. They clambered onto their chairs, flapping their arms wildly, and landed with a bump on the floor.

They went and sat down again.

That's easy, sitting!

"Do you know what I'm thinking, Warren?" said Tina suddenly. "Birdy has no arms. And she has no hands. That means she'll never be able to play the piano. But we could, if we knew how."

"Which do you think would be more enjoyable?" asked Warren. "Playing the piano or flying?"

"Both would be lovely," said Tina, "especially if you could do them straight away, without having to learn how to first."

Together they mulled over the many things it would be wonderful to do, without having to learn how to do them first. Imagine waking up one fine day to realize, hey, I can do that. And saying to each other, "Look what I can suddenly do!"

"I can speak ten languages at the same time."

"I can run all day without getting tired or tripping!"

"I can play five musical instruments at once!"

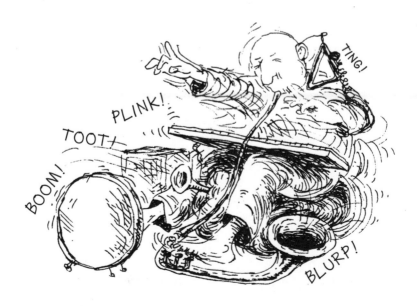

"I'm thirsty," said Warren suddenly.

"I can make a cup of tea," said Tina, and she went to the kitchen.

Birdy came and stood by the kitchen chairs. She looked at Warren. Her face went very red. Her wings flapped up and down.

And she said something she hadn't said before. "Peep-peep!"

6

"Did you hear that?" Warren called out towards the kitchen. "She said *peep-peep*. So she really is a bird."

Tina hurried back into the room.

"She said *peep-peep*? *Peep-peep*? Well then, she was trying to say *Papa*. Did you say it first? Was she trying to imitate you? She said *Papa*!"

Birdy sat on the floor. Her face went all red again. Tina and Warren watched closely. Something was happening inside her. A balloon full of letters was set to burst. A puff of air in the shape of a word.

It was coming. They strained to hear. Yes, here it came.

"Meep-meep!"

"Did you hear that? Did you?" cried Tina. "She's saying *Mama*! She's just having a little bit of trouble with the *a*."

Birdy repeated the words.

"Peep-peep! Meep-meep!"

All day long.

It got easier.

"Peep-peep. Meep-meep. Peep-peep. Meep-meep. Peep-peep. Meep-meep. Eep."

Two days later, at about quarter past one, when Tina was home by herself and the wind was blowing and it was a Thursday, Birdy suddenly and unexpectedly said, "I weent a seendweech weeth peeneet beettee."

"What did you say?" asked Tina.

"I weent a seendweech weeth peeneet beettee."

"I understand, I understand!" exclaimed Tina above the sound of the wind. She raced to the kitchen and made a sandwich, spreading it thickly with peanut butter.

She ended up with a lot of the peanut butter smeared onto the table and her fingers. She licked the remains off the butter-knife so vigorously that she made her cheeks brown and sticky. Trying to keep calm, she cut the sandwich into small pieces and fed it piece by piece to Birdy.

"You can talk," she said. "How marvelous! Although it's still baby talk because you aren't saying the all the letters properly yet. It's not seendweech but sandwich, with an *a* and an *i*. Try saying aaaaaaaaaaaaaaaaa."

"Ee," said Birdy. "Ee."

"No, it's *a*," said Tina, "aaaaaaaaaaaaaaaaaaaaaaaaaaa."

"Ee," said Birdy.

"Try saying *i* then, iiiiiiiiiiiiiiiiiiiiiiiiiiiiiiiiiiii."

"Ee," said Birdy.

"Try an *o*, ooooooooooooooooooooooooo."

"Ee," said Birdy.

"Try *u*, uuuuuuuuuuuuuuuuuuuuuuuuuuu."

"U," said Birdy.

"Excellent!" exclaimed Tina. "That's much better. "But now, how about aaaaa?"

Birdy said nothing.

"Can you say your name?" asked Tina.

Birdy said nothing.

"Come on, just try it once: Birdy, Birdy, Birdy."

"B…B…Beedy."

That evening Warren arrived home with his bird book and binoculars.

"We've been practicing," said Tina. "But she can't say *i* and *r*. She can't say her own name. That's no good, Warren, because if you can't say your own name you can't say who you are. She said Beedy instead of Birdy, so she'd better be called Beedy."

"Well, why not," said Warren. "Beedy it is then."

So, from then on, Birdy was called Beedy.

7

Warren and Tina were at the table eating soup. Alphabet noodle soup. They were fishing for words. Whenever they caught a word, they ate it up.

Tina ate "put" and "wood" and "so". Warren ate "miss" and "vet" and "kiss". And by accident, "fon," which didn't mean anything, but tasted nice all the same.

"Warren?" said Tina, all of a sudden.

"Mmm?" said Warren.

"Our Beedy has a speech impediment."

"So do lots of people," said Warren. "Thum have trouble thaying the letter *s*. They lithp. Other people have twouble saying the letter *r*. There's nothing really the matter with them."

"But she doesn't have any hands either. You can't get very far in life without hands and with a speech impediment, can you?"

"You don't have to worry about a bird's future."

"But she's not a bird! Birds don't say 'I weent a seendweech weeth peeneet beettee'. They just don't! What's going to become of her, Warren? We're not sure what she is. She'll never know where she came from. She doesn't have any hands, *and* she has a speech impediment."

"But she has wings, doesn't she?" said Warren.

Without warning, Tina began to cry into her soup. Her tears made round ripples in the soup bowl. All in the shape of the letter *o*.

"Couldn't you have found a normal child?" she said. "One with arms, like I have. One that everyone could look at and admire and say: 'Wow, doesn't she look just like you?' Why couldn't you have found a child like that? What on earth are wings good for?"

"You can do a lot with wings," said Warren soothingly. "There are always things to be done up high. Delivering airmail letters, for instance. Keeping an eye on things."

"What sort of things?"

"I don't know exactly. What I do know is that there are lots of things that have to be done up high, and they would be a doddle to do with wings."

"Really?"

"Really. Beedy has something that nobody else has."

"Fof," said Tina.

"What?"

"Fof. I'm going to eat the word 'fof'".

And that she did. With her mouth shut.

8

Warren was out and about again, identifying birds, making sure they matched up with their descriptions in his book. It was years since Tina had gone with him. She had, once, but she'd only been allowed to hold the binoculars for a short time and never the book.

Tina stayed at home with Beedy. She quickly forgot what life was like before Beedy came into it. These days she was always busy with Beedy. She helped her learn to talk, starting with short sentences that disguised Beedy's speech impediment. For example:

The bee sleeps here.

Three peek at a neat leaf.

Tina tried to toilet train Beedy, but Beedy didn't want to be toilet trained. She preferred to use the yard. They had to leave a window open so Beedy could go out whenever she needed.

Tina taught Beedy table manners.

She put a spoon between her wings, but it fell to the ground.

She put the spoon between her toes, but then Beedy couldn't get it to her mouth.

Next, Tina made an especially elongated spoon. Finally, after a big struggle, Beedy managed to eat a few mouthfuls of food by herself.

"Eep, meep-meep, eep!" Beedy said. She flapped onto the china cabinet. She stayed up there, looking down.

"Come back," said Tina. "You haven't finished eating, so you can't leave the table yet."

"Eek," said Beedy.

"That's just the way it is," said Tina.

"Ees," said Beedy.

"Oh you! Be a good girl and come down now. We're not very good company for each other with you up there and me down here."

Beedy fluttered back down.

"Now, back at the table," Tina encouraged her.

But Beedy scrabbled around the floor, bending down from time to time to slurp something up. A small spider about to eat its own meal. An earwig that had lost its way.

"Gracious, what are you doing?" cried Tina.

"Yeem yeem," said Beedy.

"Spit it out. You don't eat things off the floor. Spit it out."

But Beedy had already swallowed the insects.

She found them delicious.

9

Warren came home later than usual. There had been a lot of birds around that day, and plenty of other things as well, like kites, model planes and pollen. Especially pollen.

"I've had a busy day," said Warren.

"Me too," said Tina. "I taught Beedy to use silverware. Well, just a spoon actually. I'll show you."

She fetched a plate and took it outside. She returned a few minutes later. On the plate were a couple of earthworms with a spider for garnish.

"She enjoys these even more than peanut butter," said Tina. "At first I thought it was pretty disgusting, but I'm getting used to it. After all, we eat rump steak, chicken wings, snails and suchlike."

She sat Beedy at the table and held onto her. She wedged the extra-long spoon between Beedy's toes and placed a worm on it. Beedy ate the worm using the spoon. But as soon as Tina let go of her, Beedy leaned forward and gulped up the rest straight off the plate.

"She *can* do it," said Tina.

"But listen, Tina," said Warren, "if Beedy carries on eating this way she'll always have her feet on the table. How can we take her to a nice restaurant if she does that? She won't be able to bury her face in the plate either."

That was true. People always sat up straight at the table when they were eating. Even though it was possible to eat in other ways.

In a quick way

or in a slobby way.

In a lazy way

or in a clumsy way.

"Hang on," said Warren, "I'll make something so she can sit up like a person and still eat like a bird."

He went straight to his shed. He was busily occupied for the next two hours. Tina wasn't allowed to come and watch what he was doing. She definitely couldn't come and ask if he was finished yet even though she was ready to dish up the soup.

When Warren returned he was very pleased with himself. He had made a wind-controlled eating apparatus. "Not made, but *constructed*," he said because that sounded more impressive. He felt sure this was the world's first wind-controlled eating apparatus, though he had traveled to only two other countries.

They tried it out immediately. Beedy had to flutter and flap without lifting off in order to create enough wind. Wind made the contraption work.

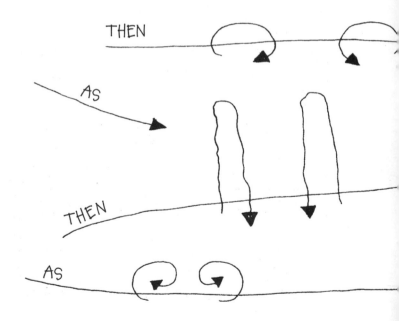

It was hard work for Beedy's wings and sometimes she forgot to keep standing in the right position.

On the other hand, creating the wind made her wings stronger. They developed into wings to be proud of.

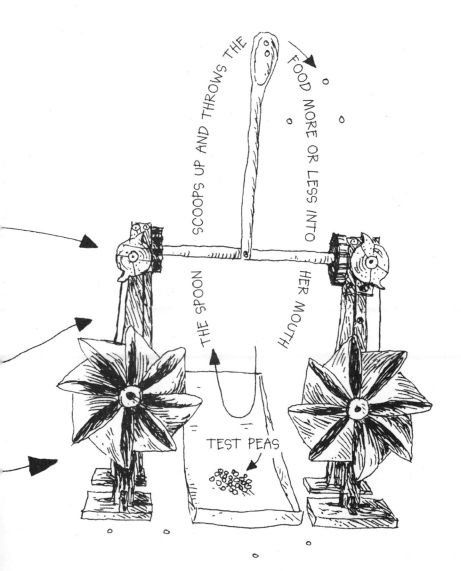

SCOOPS UP AND THROWS THE

FOOD MORE OR LESS INTO

THE SPOON

HER MOUTH

TEST PEAS

"Come on," Tina said to Beedy one day, "why don't we go into town? You're so good at walking now. I've bought you a pair of lovely red shoes. And I've made you a new, sky blue jacket cape. But remember not to use your wings."

She fetched the new jacket cape and draped it over Beedy's shoulders. She brought out the new shoes and put them on Beedy's feet.

"They look perfect," she said.

Tina was the one who couldn't stop admiring the shoes. Even after they arrived in town, she kept looking at them. At their lovely, rippling redness.

Tina kept hold of Beedy's jacket cape. You couldn't see that Beedy had no arms. She looked just like any other little girl with a mother and a pair of red shoes.

They didn't meet anyone who knew them. For that reason no one said *Good morning* or *Look who's here*. On the other hand, there were plenty of friendly notices in shop windows that said things like *Welcome* and *Thank you* and *Come again.*

They sauntered past the shop fronts. From time to time Tina stopped to window shop. She picked out the nicest and the tastiest things, but she didn't buy any of them.

Beedy's new shoes began to pinch. She walked slower and slower. It took Tina a while to realize that the shoes were the problem.

"Let's have a break," she said, when she finally became aware of it.

They went into a big café and sat down at one of the tables. Tina ordered a cup of tea for herself. It tasted a little of ancient forest. A piece of chocolate had melted on the saucer. Beedy had a glass of lemonade with a straw. She didn't need hands to drink from the straw.

The walls and ceiling of the big café were one huge landscape painting. It was almost like picnicking outside. Above their heads, chubby, naked, winged cherubs brushed against the painted sky. They seemed to be holding the ceiling up so it wouldn't fall down on top of the customers. The ceiling sky was also decorated with stars, so that it looked like day and night at the same time.

Beedy couldn't stop staring at the painting. She became very agitated.

"Flee," she said. "Free." Nervously she began to flutter her wings.

"Keep still, keep still," hissed Tina. "If anyone notices that you have wings you'll never be able to go out for lemonade again."

But Beedy couldn't help herself. She kept on flexing her wings.

Tina became very agitated, too. She began to think that everyone was watching her, that everyone would be able to see the wings through the jacket cape and that they'd come up to her and say, "It's no use trying to hide them. We've seen them now. We're taking her to the police. Or the zoo." Or words to that effect. Very upsetting in any case.

"What's the matter?" Tina said to Beedy. "Do you have to pee? Come on, then. You can't go outside, not here. For once you'll have to use a proper toilet."

She took hold of Beedy's jacket cape and led her to the restrooms. Behind a door that said "Ladies" was a small room with mirrors and, beyond that, the toilet cubicle. Luckily no one else was there so Beedy could stretch her wings.

"Go and have a pee now," said Tina. She helped Beedy onto the seat and waited in the small room, guarding the cubicle door that Beedy wasn't able to lock.

Another lady came inside.

"Are you in line?" the lady said.

"More or less," said Tina.

"You know," said the lady, "I always go to the bathroom just before I really need to because once you're desperate then you can't wait, and more often than not you do have to wait. So I'd rather not wait until I really need to go. What do you think?"

"I've never thought about it like that," said Tina. "If I need to go, then I need to go, and I do."

"That's true too," said the lady, "but it's a bit of a business, isn't it? A few times a day stuff goes in and stuff comes out. Oh well, at least we still have plenty of time for other things, don't we? Many animals spend their whole day on nothing else."

The lady had a spot on her cheek. She peered at it very closely in one of the mirrors, twisting her mouth right down so she could get a good look. The shape of her mouth was now much more noticeable than the spot.

"Now I really have to go," she said. "Isn't she done yet?"

Tina checked to see if Beedy had finished. She put her head round the cubicle door. Then she opened the door wide.

She saw the toilet bowl.

She saw the closed lid of the toilet bowl.

She saw two red shoes, one beside the other, on the closed lid of the toilet bowl.

She saw an open window above the two red shoes on the closed lid of the toilet bowl. The opening was too narrow for a big person but wide enough for a small one.

Beyond the window she saw the blue sky.

The big, empty blue sky.

The much too big, far too empty blue sky.

"Beedy!" she cried. "Don't fly away. I don't want you to fly away."

But it was too late. Beedy couldn't hear her anymore.

11

That evening, when Warren returned from his birdwatching, he called out: "Tina! I've just seen another bird like our Beedy. So there *is* another one. As blue as the sky."

He stopped talking when he saw Tina just sitting there. She looked dejected and pale, although her eyes were red: as red as the little red shoes on the floor.

"That blue," he stammered. "Was it…? But…? How…? Or wasn't it…?"

"Yes, it was," snuffled Tina. "You've guessed right."

He sat next to her on a kitchen chair. They put their arms around one another.

"Oh, Warren," said Tina.

"Oh, Tina," said Warren.

"There was nothing I could do," Tina sobbed.

"You can't stop birds flying away," said Warren. "It's what they do. One day, they just take off."

"But it's much too soon. She doesn't even know how to boil an egg yet and there were still so many songs I wanted to teach her."

The eating apparatus stood beside the table, superfluous. It was such a marvelous invention, too.

A delectable spider was creeping up to the ceiling.

"Do you think I should never have brought her home with me?" asked Warren.

"Yes, of course you should've. Otherwise I'd never have

known what I was missing out on. I'd wondered about that. What was I missing? Now I know."

She picked up a feather that was dancing over the floor.

"Did you feel how soft her feathers were on the inside of her wings?" she asked.

"Yes," said Warren. "They were lovely and soft."

"And she could already say so much."

"Yes, a lot."

"Well."

"Ahh."

They were silent for a little while. Eventually Warren said, "If we had wings as well, we could follow her."

But most people who had ever tried to make wings had fallen back to earth. Their wings were home-made. And they didn't work.

12

Far away, and shoeless, Beedy soared through the air. From land, she looked like a large bird of prey. And birds of prey are protected. People leave them alone.

Beneath her she saw great forests so dense they looked as if no one ever ventured into them. She saw lakes with sailing boats on them. They sailed from one side to the other and back again without bumping into one another and without appearing to have anywhere in particular to go. She saw lots of doll-sized people but, from such a height, she couldn't tell if they were men or women.

Beedy was flying well. She seemed to be sky-swimming, doing breaststroke and backstroke. Treading the air like water.

Then she saw the city below her. She saw roofs and chimneys. She saw a park with trees. She saw church spires.

She glided down, finding a flat roof where she could rest against a chimney. The bottom of her left wing hurt, right at the back.

Next door to the flat roof was a slanting roof where a window stood open. Beedy flew towards it. She rested in the gutter for a moment, checking that all was still and peaceful inside. Seen through the window, the small room seemed empty and quiet. It had a bed and a chair, a wardrobe and a bookshelf. There were toys on the floor and big posters on the wall. Beedy fluttered inside and lay on the bed. She had to leave her jacket cape on because she couldn't undo the button with her toes.

She fell asleep right away, wrapped in the silence of the little room.

Beedy didn't notice the nice fat fly crawling over the ceiling. Or the sky slowly darkening, a bit of pea soup green mixed in with the grey. Then a girl came into the room, chasing the silence away.

The girl's name was Lottie. She noticed her visitor immediately. She saw Beedy's bare feet with their ten toes, their toenails and the smidgen of dirt under each nail.

And she saw her wings.

She wasn't a bit surprised. Lottie had always believed she'd have a special visitor sooner or later. She'd wished very hard that, one day, someone or something extraordinary would be waiting for her when she got home.

Someone like this perhaps.

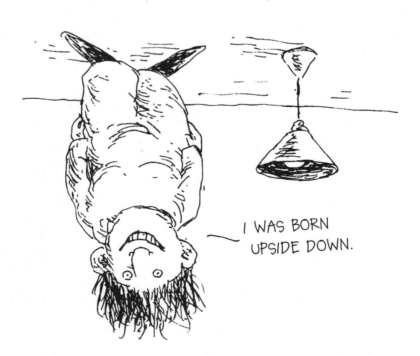

I WAS BORN UPSIDE DOWN.

Or like this.

Or this.

And now it had finally happened. Now she knew that some wishes came true.

When she tried to see if the wings came off, she woke Beedy.

"Hi," said Lottie. "I wished for you."

"Eep," said Beedy.

"You must have flown inside."

"Meep-meep," said Beedy.

"I thought so," said Lottie. "They're on pretty tight. That's good. If your wings came off, you'd fall down."

"Peep-peep."

"I hope you won't have to leave just as soon as you've arrived," said Lottie, "because that would be a shame. If my father saw you, you'd have to leave. I don't want that to happen. What's your name?"

"Beedy," said Beedy.

"I'm Lottie."

Lottie lived with her father. He was a very busy man. Sometimes it seemed to Lottie as if he had to be responsible for everything. Keeping the traffic on the proper side of the road. Making sure that the autumn leaves were swept away before winter. Stopping houses from falling over. Everything. He was a man who worried a lot, something his balding head and rumpled trousers seemed to prove. He didn't have time for visitors. Often he didn't have much time for Lottie either.

He would say to Lottie, "I don't have time for you right now," when, in fact, Lottie could have saved him time by being useful in all sorts of ways.

AS A CHRISTMAS TREE, PERHAPS

OR AS A CRUMB-COLLECTOR

"Where did you get your wings from?" asked Lottie.

"Eep," said Beedy.

"Probably from overseas."

Lottie had never seen anyone in her neighborhood with wings. But she wasn't at all surprised that there were such people. She knew, from watching television, that there were people who could turn a man into a woman, or vice versa. That they could cross peaches with plums, and perhaps berries with apples as well, so they'd end up with pluches and berples, or something like that. And she knew they could attach loose fingers and legs and bits of skin wherever they wanted. Up close on television, she's seen them sew a severed finger back on. Because it had been filmed so close-up she hadn't been able to see exactly *where* the finger had been sewn back. Probably somewhere not too noticeable.

So, not on someone's forehead

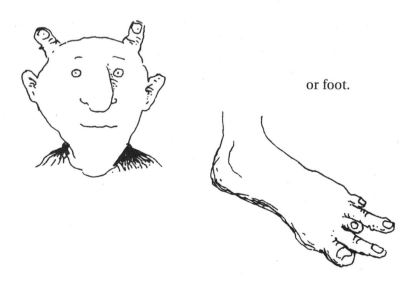

or foot.

Beedy sat up straight. She fluttered her wings briefly to get her balance.

Then she took a deep breath and said, "I weent a seendweech weeth peeneet beettee."

Lottie looked at her. She understood.

She said, "I've fanished the peanat batter. But I've got some chaca-spread."

She went downstairs and made a couple of sandwiches, one for Beedy and one for herself. She cut them up small, since her visitor didn't have any hands.

As soon as Beedy got her sandwich she bent over and sucked up a mouthful. Lottie wanted to eat like that too, but every time she managed to grab a piece with her lips, another piece stuck to her nose.

"I want to keep you," Lottie said.

And she closed the roof window.

13

Together Warren and Tina walked through the countryside near their house. Tina had found that she felt so alone now whenever Warren was away. Staying at home by herself was suddenly too hard. Beedy was far too clearly *not there*. Not at the table, not on the china cabinet, not in the basket. She was so completely *nowhere* that Tina couldn't stop thinking about her not being there.

For that reason she preferred to be out birdwatching with Warren.

Warren didn't mind at all. He let Tina carry the binoculars and the bird book. Looking up into the sky, however, wasn't such a good idea. Their sadness was bigger than the sky.

They decided to go into town. There were lots of other people there, people they didn't know and didn't have to talk to. But at least it was better than nothing and no one. And, in town, they could buy themselves a sweet treat to eat. Sweet treats were comforting. Of course, a pat on the head could be comforting as well. Perhaps a pat on the head *with* a sweet treat would be doubly comforting, but people didn't usually combine the two.

When they arrived in town they went to a café, one with soft seats and inviting tablecloths. They took their time studying the menu. If you chose something and then changed your mind when it was too late, it was no longer as comforting.

They chose a large custard square each. Cheerful, yellow custard slid easily down the throat. And they each asked for a cup of coffee with dollops of cream.

Now they had plenty to keep them busy, making sure the pastry stayed on the fork without falling apart, ensuring the custard didn't wobble off the fork. Avoiding getting a cream mustache. Dabbing up crumbs with a damp finger before chewing them into even smaller crumbs.

"Warren," said Tina.

"Yes," said Warren.

"I can understand that she needed to fly away since that's a feeling that comes from deep inside, but couldn't she have said *Goodbye* and *See you later* or something along those lines: *Geedbee* and *See yee leeder*. Now she's gone and she never said goodbye."

"Yes," said Warren. "But perhaps birds don't know they're supposed to say that."

"But I taught her that we say *Goodbye* and *Enjoy your meal* and *How are you?* and *May I get past?* If she had to fly away I couldn't have stopped her, but I'd really have liked—I'd *really* have liked—to have said, *Goodbye, go if you must*, and then let her go. That would have been like a full stop at the end of a sentence. If there's a full stop, then you can start a new sentence. If there isn't, then the sentence hasn't come to an end, and you don't know for sure…then you always keep on…then you think…do you understand?"

"She's not here anymore, Tina."

"Can't we go and look for her? Only to say *Bon voyage* and *Come and see us sometime?*"

"How can we? Where would we start?"

"We can ask around. Someone might know where someone who flies away is able to fly to…I've read that in the city you can get all sorts of information. They say that they know something about everything and that they can get answers from anywhere. They can get an answer from China, for example, if the answer's to be found in China. There's an unbelievable amount of information out there, just waiting for people. They'd be able to help us, wouldn't they?"

"Yes, but then we'd have to explain about the wings," said Warren. "We wouldn't be able to keep them a secret any longer."

"We'll have to ask the question so that they understand us but don't really know what we mean; do you follow? Surely we can do that. I mean, I don't always understand everything but I still understand a little bit of it."

"Yes, I know," said Warren. But really, he didn't understand at all.

Tina picked up something else from her plate with a damp finger. She ate it. Warren saw it was a very small sort of fly. She seemed to enjoy it.

14

"I'll buy us some peanut butter," Lottie told Beedy. "Since that's what you like. You stay here. I'll be back soon. I'll look after you really well."

And she went out to buy the peanut butter. She was going to look for the biggest jars she could, ones that contained the smoothest peanut butter as well as real peanut pieces.

Beedy stayed behind by herself. At first she scrabbled around the floor a bit. She found insects under the bed but they were thick with dust and no longer fresh. Then she began to flutter around, faster and faster. She fluttered against the roof window, which was shut. She fluttered into the door, which was also closed. And against the bookcase. School books fell off. Beedy's small left toe started to bleed slightly after her collision with the bookcase. In fright she dropped a little poop on the floor. Then, tired of everything, she lay back on the bed. The bottom of her left wing was hurting again, right at the back.

"Eep, eep, eep," she chirruped to the clouds outside.

Lottie finally came back with two jars of peanut butter that looked quite ordinary.

"What have you done now?" she asked. She fetched a paper towel, scooped up the small poop and threw the towel into the trash can. She picked up the books from the floor. Some of them were from when she was learning to write. Whole rows of a's and o's. Beedy couldn't pronounce them. Perhaps you needed arms and hands to be able to say them properly. That must be why so many people waved their arms and hands about when they were standing around talking.

There were well drawn a's and o's.

And there were badly drawn a's and o's.

The best way of using those was to turn them into completely new letters, for sounds that didn't have letters of their own yet. There were lots of sounds that didn't have their own letters yet. Sounds with a lot of spit in them. Or sounds that you made when you breathed in, or when you stuck your tongue out.

Lottie looked in another exercise book. She'd been allowed to take them all home when the holidays began.

In that book she'd written that sandy soil was poor soil. It was something she'd learned, that sandy soil was a sorry sort of soil. But the beach was full of sand that you could make sand castles with. There was nothing wrong with that. Except when the sand castles collapsed. Then you felt sorry for the poor sand.

Just then Lottie heard her father coming up the stairs.

"Quick," she hissed. "Under my bed."

She picked Beedy up and pushed her under the bed, like a package.

Her father came inside. He was tall, very tall. He almost reached the ceiling. He never looked under the bed. To do that, he would have to fold himself up too much.

He told her that the meal was ready. It was macaroni cheese with ham and it had been made in a hurry. He also said that the next day he had to go away again to organize a lot of things. He was going to be gone a week, he thought. The babysitter would come and stay.

The babysitter stayed whenever Lottie's father was away. She was a very busy woman who was studying in order to improve herself. She made instant meals. Lottie always got a full plate. She was also allowed to eat in front of the television, something her father never let her do. She enjoyed that, except if there was a bloody operation being shown in close-up. Then she quickly lost her appetite.

15

The following day Warren and Tina took the train to the city. Tina carried a large bag containing things that might come in useful. Packable raincoats, even though it hadn't rained for ages. Folding umbrellas and fold-up sun hats. They both stared out of the window at the sky. It was blue but bereft of Beedy.

The city center was packed with people. There was hardly room to move. People were out hunting for clothes and perfume and music and toothpaste. Warren and Tina had no idea where to get the information they needed. It wasn't just going to be on display for them in a store window.

They came to a sudden stop beside a wall of glass. Other shoppers bumped into them before detouring around. On the floor behind the glass wall stood a large plant that looked like a fragment of ancient forest. Alongside the plant, women were sitting behind computers.

"Information," said a notice above the women's heads.

"There you go," said Warren. "Information. This must be one of those places where you can ask anything."

They went inside. The women smiled. The floor shone.

"How can I help you?" one of them inquired. Her nose shone as well.

Warren and Tina wanted to explain about Beedy but, at the same time, they didn't want to give too much away. They had no idea how to say something without actually saying it.

"Ah...we're searching for..." Tina began. "It's to do with flying away without saying goodbye."

The woman looked at them. Then she said, "If it's about flying, we have a number of special-rate package vacations."

"But it's more about not knowing where to go..."

"I can give you brochures about all our trips," the woman offered. She plonked a pile of brochures in front of Tina.

"You can go anywhere you like. Africa, South America, Australia. You'll find there are beaches to sunbathe everywhere. And when you pay for a trip you'll receive a free beach towel, as well as two handy booklets with information about all the beaches and the shops."

"We don't really need that kind of information," Warren tried to explain. "It's not about that sort of flying, you see."

"What sort is it then?" the woman asked.

"It's about..." said Warren, "that's to say, um, it's about, ah, it's more about a bird than a plane. Much more. Actually."

"But still more about a person than a bird," Tina added.

"I'm afraid I can't help you there," said the woman, as politely as she could. Then she started inspecting her fingernails.

Warren and Tina went back outside.

"We didn't explain ourselves clearly enough," said Warren.

"I thought I could explain without really explaining," said Tina, "but when I try it doesn't really mean anything to anybody else."

"They'll never be able to help us search if they don't know what we're looking for. Perhaps we'd better just go home, Tina, and hope that Beedy comes back to visit us sometime. This isn't working. We have to know where to look. If she'd been in the city, and someone had seen her, she would have ended up in the newspaper, like everything unusual.

"Like someone discovering strange footprints

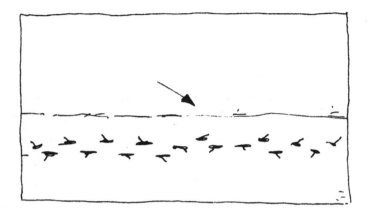

or someone taking a photo of a UFO

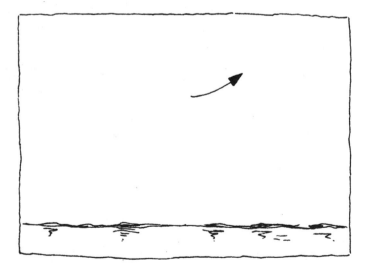

or someone thinking they've seen a monster."

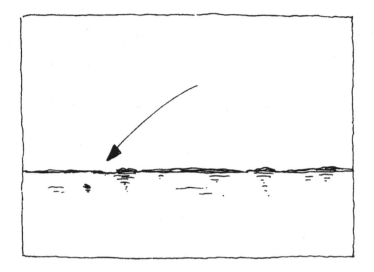

"How can you give up when we haven't even started looking properly yet," Tina protested. "We've only just arrived in the city."

"Well, we've made a small start already," said Warren. "But you're right, let's begin in earnest."

So they pushed on, parting the sea of people who wanted to buy clothes and perfume and music and toothpaste and the daily newspaper.

They carried on trying.

16

Early in the morning, Lottie had gone to the park to collect an armful of branches. She dragged them to her bedroom. She stripped the sheets off the bed then gathered up all the house-plants from all the windowsills in the house and put them around the branches on the floor. The houseplants hadn't been watered for a while.

"I've made a nest," she said. "I want to be a bird, too. Then I won't have to go to school anymore."

Beedy had to sit in the nest. Lottie sat in it as well. It was hard and prickly, even with the sheets. She got out again, remember-ing she'd forgotten something. Eggs. There were still a couple in the fridge. She put the eggs into the nest as carefully as she could. But as she clambered back in, also as carefully as she could, she fell on top of them. Now there was a slimy, gooey mix of egg white and yolk on her clothes. Trying to wipe it away didn't help.

Suddenly she heard a clumping sound on the stairs. It was her tall father with his big feet in his heavy shoes. He was coming upstairs again.

She grabbed Beedy and pushed her rather roughly under the bed.

"Don't move!" she ordered.

"What a mess!" her father said as soon as he stepped inside.

"It's a nest," said Lottie.

"You'll clean it up when you've finished playing, won't you?"

"I won't be finished for ages."

"You know I have to get going," said her father. "The baby-sitter's not coming until seven, so you'll be by yourself for a couple of hours. Am I going to get a kiss goodbye?"

Lottie kissed him on a prickly part. She got three kisses in return. Her father had lifted her up so he could reach her face more easily.

Lottie warned him, "I'm not very good at hatching eggs yet."

"Heavens above!" cried her father. "What's that muck?"

"It's from an egg I laid," said Lottie. "In my nest."

"That's foul! My best suit, too. I'll have to clean it now. Why do you always do things like this?"

"Eep," said Lottie.

Her father looked even more burdened than usual. He tried to go back to his usual self but it didn't work.

"Say goodbye to Daddy."

"Eep," said Lottie.

"Come on, say goodbye. I'm going to be away for a whole week."

"Eep!"

"Can't you say goodbye properly?"

Her father went off down the hall in his heavy shoes, muttering words that Lottie couldn't quite hear.

She went back to her nest. Somewhere in the house, she heard a tap running.

Not long afterwards the front door was pulled shut.

"Bye," she called out through the closed roof window.

There was a pigeon sitting there. Perhaps he could hear her.

17

Birds don't live in houses. They belong outside.

Lottie had written a note to the babysitter.

> You don't have to babysit me.
> I'm going to be staying with
> someone else. I'll call you
> when I come back.   Lottie.

She went out the door, taking Beedy with her. The front door key was hanging on a string round her neck. Under her arm she carried a blanket that kept trying to slip away. Beedy wore shoes that were too small for Lottie. They were too big for Beedy.

"We're going to go to a real tree," said Lottie. "We're real birds. But we'll have to walk there like ordinary people. Otherwise we'll be noticed."

So they walked down the street like ordinary people. No one noticed the wings under Beedy's jacket cape. And Beedy kept her feet as close to the ground as possible, otherwise her shoes would have fallen off.

They went to the park. Amongst the very many ordinary trees, one stood out. This one was old and spreading. Its branches resembled strong arms that could embrace you in a reassuring hug.

The spaces where trunk and branches met were like giant armpits, snug hollows big enough to sit in.

"Get into the tree," whispered Lottie.

"Eep, peep-peep, eep!"

Beedy flew into the tree and there she stayed, cradled in the highest armpit.

Lottie decided to stay at a lower level. She did her best to be a bird, but she didn't look like a bird. She looked more like a girl about to fall.

She made a warm nest with her blanket and wrapped herself inside it.

She fell asleep quickly, even though it wasn't going to be dark for a while. At home she would have said that she wasn't tired yet, not a bit, and why did they think she was?

Now she fell asleep, just like that.

She dreamed about her father.

She dreamed about an egg she had to hatch. She had to sit on it the whole time, even though she wanted to go away and do fun things. Hatching an egg wasn't much fun at all.

She took a close look at the egg. It was a plastic egg that opened like a little container and a present popped out.

You didn't have to hatch that sort of egg. You just opened it. Her father was sitting inside the egg. He was the surprise. He was tiny.

"I'm cold," he said.

She covered him with a blanket. But he disappeared inside its folds. She couldn't find him again.

"Daddy," she called, "Daddy. I didn't say goodbye to you!"

18

Warren and Tina had spent the whole afternoon traipsing to various businesses and other places. They'd collected a whole heap of information. They knew when the buses stopped running. They knew what was on at the movies. They knew the exchange rates. They knew when planes left for Africa. They knew what the weather was going to be like. They knew which wars were still being fought. They knew when the city first became a city. They knew which famous people were having a birthday. They knew, more or less, where the famous people lived. They knew lots more besides. But they still had no idea where Beedy had gone.

By then it was evening and too late to go home so they decided to look for a cheap hotel.

They walked up and down the streets hoping to find one. Quiet streets. Whenever they saw a sign advertising a hotel they went inside.

They asked, "Do you have a room?"

The answer was the same wherever they asked. "No." All the rooms had already been taken by people who had arrived earlier.

"I can't believe there isn't any space," said Tina, after their tenth attempt. "Did you see that lovely bench in the hallway? That's space enough."

The eleventh time, they asked if they could sleep in the hall. But they soon discovered this wasn't allowed.

"There *has* to be a spare bed somewhere," muttered Tina, "or even just somewhere we can lie down."

She knew that thinking like this wouldn't help matters.

There was no way they would be able to stay at any of the hotels.

If only they could go somewhere for information, find out if there was still a bed available.

They hadn't asked that question in any of the places they'd been to and now they were all closed.

It began to get dark.

"We'll have to sleep outside," said Warren. "There's no other choice. It's going to be a warm night, so we'll manage."

They looked for a place to sleep. If they knew someone in the city then they could just stop by and say, "Here we are!" But they didn't know anybody.

Some houses had front gardens; others had window boxes as big as beds. But everyone would see them if they tried sleeping in either of those places. They'd look like abandoned adults, far too big for anyone to want to take home with them.

Warren wondered about going to the park. They'd be able to find a quiet spot there.

"Oh Warren," said Tina, "do I have to sleep on the grass? It's such a wide, open-air bedroom."

But the park was certainly very peaceful. Amongst the very many ordinary trees, one stood out. This one was old and spreading. Its branches resembled strong arms that could embrace you in a reassuring hug. And the spaces where trunk and branches met were like giant armpits. Not that they could see this very clearly anymore, not in the dark.

Tina unpacked the packable raincoats and spread them out over the grass under the wide, safe tree.

She and Warren snuggled close together and kissed each other goodnight.

"I suddenly feel very calm," whispered Tina, "so calm...it's good here. Cheap hotels sometimes have horrible beds. You get lost in them. It's nice and airy here, too."

She sighed and drifted off into a deep sleep.

But Warren stayed awake.

He heard sounds he didn't recognize. He thought about birds and became restless. He knew so much about birds, and the more he thought about them, the harder it was to fall asleep. Somewhere he'd read that you could fall asleep if you repeated a calming sentence. If you thought about that and nothing else, then no other thought could intrude.

He knew one sentence in which nothing fluttered or flew: The slow slug sleeps in the sloppy salad.

He repeated the sentence. The slow slug sleeps in the sloppy salad. The slow slug sleeps in the sloppy salad. The slow slug sleeps in the sloppy salad. The slow slug sleeps in the sloppy salad. The slow slug sleeps in the sloppy salad. The slow slug sleeps in the sloppy salad. The slow. Slug. Sleeeeeps. Inde. Sloppy. Sallll.

The. Slo. Slu. Sweep. Slop. Salllllll.

The. Slldeslll...Assluh...asssasss...

Sssssss...

......

(It helped.)

19

Most people were still asleep when the new day began. Some, who were still busy with the day before, came out of cafés and sleep-walked their way home. Others, who were already busy with the day ahead, left early for work. There were also others who couldn't care less what day it was. They rummaged in rubbish bins to see if anything useful had been thrown away.

Lottie was sleeping in the park close to such a rubbish bin. She dreamed about her father. He was very small and was tucked away somewhere in her blanket. "I'm choking! I can't breathe!" he cried. Lottie fought vigorously with the blanket to try to free her father. The blanket slipped off her onto the ground.

Warren lay next to Tina, asleep under the tree. He was dreaming that all sorts of things were flying through the air. Beds, buses, newspapers, a slow slug and a heap of sloppy salad. How could all those things stay up in the air, he wondered. Shouldn't they fall?

And then, all of a sudden, they did fall, right on top of him.

"Arragh!" he shouted, and woke up instantly.

But the only thing that was lying on top of him was a blanket. At first, that didn't seem strange at all. But then he remembered where he was. There weren't any blankets there, only grass and morning dew and cold ground.

Tina woke up as well.

"A blanket just fell on me," Warren muttered.

"I've got aching muscles," Tina muttered back. "All of my

muscles are sore. I don't know exactly how many I have but every one of them aches."

Lottie had also woken up. She heard voices under the tree. She was afraid to look down.

"Who's there?" Warren called up.

His voice didn't sound threatening. Lottie risked a peek.

"Who are you?" she asked, carefully.

"We're two people."

"Oh. I'm one person."

"What are you doing up there?" Warren asked.

"I want to become a bird. But my nest is too hard. What about you? What are you doing?"

"We're searching," said Warren, "for a sort of someone."

"What sort of a someone?"

"That's actually a secret," said Tina. "But nobody can help us search if it stays a secret."

"I'm good at keeping secrets," said Lottie. "I've got at least ten."

She swung her way out of the tree.

"If you promise not to pass it on to anyone, then I'll tell you something about it," said Tina. "But no one else is allowed to know, okay? You want to become a bird but we're talking about someone who really does have wings. And we haven't been able to say goodbye to her."

"Oh, I know all about that secret," said Lottie. "I've got someone who has wings. She's asleep high up in this tree. And she's a secret, too. She's my number-ten secret. But the biggest one."

Warren and Tina sat up quickly.

"I have to see this," said Warren.

He climbed up, disappearing amid the leaves.

"Warren, don't fall," Tina called out helpfully.

Warren didn't fall. After a moment, two shoes came down. Shoes that were too small for Lottie. Shoes that had been too big for Beedy. And then, hard on the heels of the shoes, came Warren.

"There's nothing else," he said.

Lottie began to cry. She was so overcome by sadness that she couldn't speak properly. It was as if she'd bottled up lots of other sadness, too. Now her tears spilled over. Tina tried talking to her about all kinds of different things but all she could say in reply was *sniffle-iff-iff-iff* or *blubbalubbalub* or *bwaaaaaaah*.

Warren and Tina waited until she had calmed down a little.

Then they asked her about wings where arms should be, about ten toes and a blue jacket cape, about Peep-peep and Eep. And if the number-ten secret was called Beedy.

Tina dipped into her bag and brought out two red shoes.

"Look," she said. "She really belonged to us. We found her under a bush."

"But she belonged to me as well," said Lottie, "since I found her on my bed."

Two pairs of small shoes stood on the grass.

"Perhaps she's still close by," said Warren.

"I never even said goodbye to her," said Lottie.

"Neither did we. That's why we're searching for her. Because it helps if you can say goodbye."

"Can I help search?" asked Lottie.

"You can, as far as we're concerned," said Warren, "except we don't know where to look. That's the problem. We don't know where to start.'

20

Beedy wasn't far away. She was sitting in the wide gutter of a
nearby roof. There was water in it and tasty, creeping insects.
There was also some old bread someone had thrown away.

Beedy leaned over, her tummy in the water, and slurped up
her breakfast. Her face and jacket cape became wet.

Then she sat back comfortably against the roof tiles. Her legs
dangled down.

She watched the sun rise above the houses. It would dry her. Beneath her everything was still in shadow.

As the sun crept higher many people crawled out of bed to go to work. As always, there were a lot of things to do.

More and more people walked and rode down the street, far below Beedy's dangling legs.

Some, however, stopped and looked up. Eventually more and more people did the same. That's the way it goes. If someone is staring upwards, then someone else thinks there must be something worth seeing and they look up, too. Then someone else does the same, and someone else, and someone else. Before you know it half the world is looking up, hoping it's not all a waste of time.

There were people who were certain that they could see two legs dangling over the gutter. They were terrified that the person who was sitting there was planning to jump down, so he no longer had to feel alive (which is something quite different from people who jump because they want to feel *more* alive).

There were also people who said it wasn't true about the legs. According to those people, the legs were two limp, rubbishy rags swaying in the wind. And nothing to worry about. That's also the way of the world. People can see exactly the same thing yet see it completely differently.

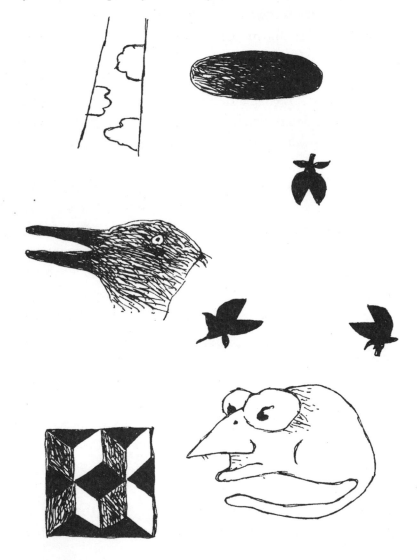

"But there's a child up there!" someone yelled. "Do something. The child's going to fall. The child has to be rescued!"

Suddenly everyone became very nervous. And everyone hoped someone else would do something. The office building on top of which the child was sitting hadn't opened for business yet. It wasn't due to open for another three minutes and every minute counted. Someone alerted the rescue service. A red and white car was heard, sirens blaring, but just before it arrived the sirens were switched off because a child up in the gutter could take fright. That had to be avoided otherwise she might really fall.

A man stepped out and called up with a loudspeaker. "Stay there. Stay there!"

Beedy became aware of the hubbub. She heard someone call, "Stay there. Stay there!" She hadn't been planning to do anything else. She wanted to dry out in the sun. But she wasn't going to stay if there was going to be too much commotion.

Someone else opened the entrance to the office building. All the curious people were herded down a side street. No one was allowed to stand beneath the gutter. Except for the rescue service personnel. And only one rescuer, the best in town, was allowed inside the building. He took the elevator to the top, eventually poking his head out of a roof window, a short distance from Beedy.

"Keep calm," he said nervously. "I'm here to rescue you. Life is beautiful."

"Peeneets!" cried Beedy.

The rescuer pulled his head back in. He prided himself on his rescuing skills. He collected everything he needed: a brightly colored rope, a stick with a little hand, and something else, a little hard to recognize, which he was sure would come in useful.

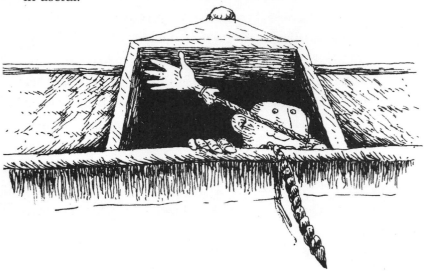

But as far as Beedy was concerned, there was too much of a stir going on. It was too difficult to settle down and dry off. She pulled in her legs, stood up and flew away in a graceful curve above the roofs, in a south-south-west direction.

The rescuer took a deep breath and crawled onto the wide gutter.

When he looked up he got a terrible shock. His legs began to tremble dangerously.

"I'm too late," he cried. "I've never been too late before. Never!" He was thrown into complete confusion. He stood in the gutter, shaking. He himself would have fallen if two other rescuers hadn't arrived in the nick of time to rescue the rescuer who had been about to do the rescue.

21

Warren, Tina and Lottie left the park. Lottie had told them they could wash and have breakfast at her place. She had the key. The hallway floor creaked. The morning sun shone onto the kitchen bench.

The babysitter was sitting in the room. She wasn't studying. She was watching Capital City Breakfast TV. Tina and Warren joined her.

"Why are you here?" asked Lottie.

"I'm babysitting," said the babysitter.

"But I wasn't here for you to babysit," said Lottie.

"It's my job to babysit so that's what I'm doing. I'm baby-sitting the doors and the plates and the tables."

"Honestly, you don't have to," said Lottie. "You're allowed to go. I'm going to be with these people and I'll be back before my father gets home."

"That's fine," said the babysitter, "as long as I get paid for the whole week. Have a good day then."

She stood up. Someone on the TV was demonstrating arm exercises.

Warren and Tina also wished her a good day.

Then they went off for a wash. Lottie didn't waste much time on getting clean. She didn't think she was very dirty. She splashed some water around in the way she imagined birds did.

Then they ate breakfast together. There weren't any eggs left but there was plenty of peanut butter.

Tina prepared coffee. While they were drinking it, she and Warren could decide what they were going to do next. Perhaps go home and carry on with life.

While the coffee was percolating, Lottie showed them a few of her favorite things, items she would inherit from her father.

He had already promised her those things, although he wasn't ready to die yet.

And she showed them the photos of when she was little, a time she couldn't remember any more.

They drank coffee. Lottie had water. They watched television since they'd run out of things to say.

Then, suddenly, the roof gutter appeared on the screen. The roof gutter minus legs. Tina and Warren took no notice. To them it was just an ordinary roof gutter.

"This is where it happened," said a reporter.

They showed an even closer shot of the gutter. It was impossible to see that anything had happened there.

Then a whole lot of people came into view. They were talking to one another.

"I was the first to see it," someone called.

"No, I'd seen it already," said another.

They were talking about a child's legs in the roof gutter.

Tina and Warren, sipping their coffee, heard *that*. They stopped sipping straight away.

There was yet another close-up, of a step this time. You could see a crumpled up shopping list lying there.

"This is where the child *would* have landed," said the reporter, "if it had fallen, which it didn't. Witnesses say that it was snatched by a bird of prey. They saw something blue being taken away."

"That must have been Beedy!" cried Tina. "Beedy's still in the city."

The front of a house came into the picture. You could see it was Number 20. There were lots of houseplants in the front window.

A reporter stood outside.

"The rescuer is inside," he said, "distressed. He doesn't want to be a rescuer any more. Unfortunately we're not allowed to film inside, even though the whole city wants to hear what the rescuer saw. It must have been dreadful. He must have witnessed a ghastly bird of prey unexpectedly appear from behind the roof. Just as he was about to rescue the child, the poor mite seems to have been snatched from his grasp and taken up into the sky. There's every chance that the child was eaten up, somewhere outside the city. We will do everything we can to keep you up-to-date with this story about the devoured child. But that's all we have for now."

Once more, the camera showed the closed door and the step and the street.

"I know where that is," said Lottie. "They've got some black paving stones there. And you can't step on them. They're dangerous.'

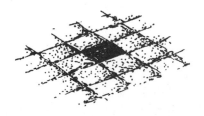

22

Lottie was very familiar with the street where the rescuer lived. It was on her way to school. There were three black paving stones. There was also a white one but it didn't count. The rest were grey.

She had told herself she wasn't allowed to step on the black paving stones because otherwise a secret trapdoor would open and she would plummet into a cellar with spirits and ghosts.

That's why she didn't like the street. But she couldn't avoid it.

Tina and Warren wanted to visit the rescuer right away. They had to talk to him in person. They had to tell him it wasn't a bird of prey, and it wasn't an ordinary child, but someone with wings and ten toes called Beedy. They had to ask the rescuer if he'd seen a blue jacket cape that covered the child as if it were hiding something.

One of the black paving stones was right in front of the rescuer's house. Beside the tile stood a photographer. He was taking photos of the house. He was trying to photograph through the window into the house using a telephoto lens, but the whole window was swathed in houseplants. All that showed up in his photos were lovely dark red flowers, magnified by the camera. And he hadn't gone there for dark red flowers.

Warren waited until the photographer disappeared round the corner. Then he rang the bell. Someone peered at them through the window.

"What do you want?" asked an elderly voice.

"We want to tell the rescuer something important," said Warren.

"He's not well."

"Maybe we can help," said Tina.

The front door opened a sliver. An old man looked them over carefully.

"You're not from the newspaper or the TV, are you?"

"Definitely not," said Tina. "We belong to ourselves."

He let them inside. The hallway smelled of macaroons.

Lottie took Tina's hand. She was scared of the cellar.

The rescuer lay on a sofa in the sitting room, his face drained of color. He eyed his three visitors suspiciously.

The drapes, patterned with large roses, were closed.

His old mother came into the room.

"Would you like some coffee?" she asked.

"Yes, please," said Tina. "No milk and two sugars."

"Me too," said Warren. "With milk and no sugar."

Lottie was allowed to have lemonade. All they had was the red sort.

"How are you?" Warren asked the rescuer.

"Bad," the rescuer said. "I've never botched a rescue before. Now it's as if all those other rescues weren't any use either. Did I rescue you once?"

"No, not me, but lots of other people, eh?" said Warren kindly. Immediately the rescuer felt a little better. He started to tell them all about who and what he had rescued during his life, including:

a bear handler who wasn't very good at his job

a dog that couldn't swim

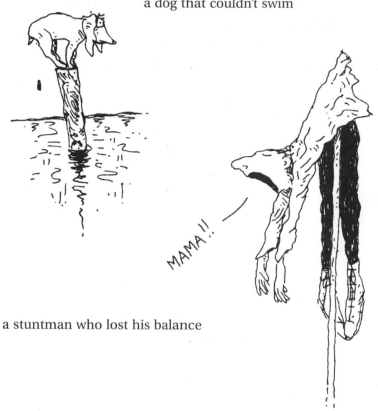

MAMA!!

a stuntman who lost his balance

and six men in a leaky boat.

After relating each story his mood improved.

"Yes, I rescued them all," he said, "but now…"

He sighed heavily.

"I don't understand any of it. There was a little girl in the gutter and I was about to rescue her. I glanced away a moment and she was gone. But no little girl had fallen to the ground. I saw something flying away. It looked like a bird of prey. I'm so scared it was a bird of prey and that it snatched the girl away to Timberbush and ate her there. She would have made a tasty little snack. And she was wearing a nice blue jacket."

"A blue jacket?" said Tina. "Then it really was Beedy."

"Are you family?" said the rescuer.

Then his elderly mother returned.

"Here you are," she said. "One lemonade, one coffee without milk and with two sugars…oh dear, I've made a mistake. This one is with milk and without coffee."

She shuffled away.

She was also rather distressed.

Warren said he had something to tell the rescuer. They hadn't told anyone else, except for Lottie.

But the rescuer had to believe them and not pass it on to anybody else.

Warren explained how he had found Beedy under a bush and how she had lived with them until she'd flown off one morning, without saying goodbye. Then Lottie explained that she'd discovered Beedy on her bed. And that Beedy had flown away a second time, again without saying goodbye.

The rescuer found all this hard to believe. He *wanted* to. He tried to.

He said, "If it's true, then it's a marvel. A miracle of nature. I want to see it for myself. If it's true, then I'll believe it. And then I'll be at peace with myself. I won't have to be worried anymore that there's an eaten-up child out there somewhere, a child I should have rescued."

"We want to see her again as well," said Tina. "To say *safe journey* and *take care* and *look after yourself.* That's why we need to know which direction she flew in."

"The bird I saw," said the rescuer, "flew in the direction of Timberbush. If that's where you're headed, can I come along? I want to see if it's true that there are still wonders in the world."

He got up off the sofa and opened the curtains. They saw the photographer dangling by his right foot from a tree.

"I'd better go and rescue him," said the rescuer.

He hurried into the backyard. First he photographed the photographer. Then he rescued him from the tree's clasp and left him outside the garden wall.

"That's that," he said when he'd finished. He called out to his elderly father and mother to tell them he was going away for a while to see if there were still wonders in the world.

"All right, son," said his parents. They could see he was already starting to get the color back in his cheeks. "But take care of yourself. And take enough clean socks. We'll make an extra big pile of well-filled sandwiches for you."

They prepared the pile of sandwiches and also filled bottles with red lemonade. The rescuer took warm sleeping bags and pillows for all four of them. He carried everything. He ended up with such a weight on his back that he was bent over.

"Isn't he strong," said his parents proudly.

They gave him three sloppy kisses. Outside the house, they waved until they lost sight of their son. Lottie was so busy waving back that she accidentally stepped on one of the black paving stones. She didn't fall into a creepy cellar. She just carried on walking without even noticing. Amazing.

23

They took a bus to the edge of the city before walking on in the direction of Timberbush.

The city didn't really know where it was supposed to end. It had a very frayed edge.

As they walked, Warren often peered through his binoculars at the sky. There were the usual varieties of birds and fluffy clouds to be seen, as well as airplanes on their way to Africa. Sometimes they'd look under a bush or into the trees.

The sky was immense and the trees and bushes seemed to carry on forever. The south-south-west also seemed endless. It was evening by the time they reached the forest.

The trees had let go the warmth of the day. The rescuer took off his pack. His back was soaked with sweat. They sat down in a hollow that was the right size for four people and unpacked their sandwiches, lifting up the corners to check what was inside them—extra thick chocolate spread and a fat layer of shoulder ham.

They ate half of the sandwiches. Lottie told them what she knew about sandy soil. Warren told them what he knew about this and that. The rescuer told them about the good feeling that rescuing gave him and how long that good feeling stayed with him before it disappeared again. Tina sang a song her mother had taught her. It was an old song so some of the words sounded a bit old-fashioned. It went like this:

Buttons, a farthing a pair!
Come, who will buy them of me?
They're round and sound and pretty,
And fit for girls of the city.
Come, who will buy them of me?
Buttons, a farthing a pair!

They sat together until their eyes grew heavy.

They decided to sleep in the hollow. Warren would be the first on look-out duty, followed by Tina and then the rescuer. Only Lottie was allowed to sleep the whole night through.

They made their beds in the hollow and said *good night* and *sleep tight* and *sweet dreams*. Warren stayed awake, listening to the forest. It shook and it shuffled and it sighed somewhat. The moon looked like an egg. The trees grew strange faces.

Before he was due to wake Tina, Warren fell asleep. In his dream he was still in the forest. He kept thinking, here comes Beedy. But then it was almost Beedy, or just about Beedy, or here and there a little bit of Beedy, but never all of her.

Suddenly he saw the real Beedy come flying towards him. He leapt up happily. "I've found you again!" he exclaimed. But behind her was another Beedy, and beside her another one, and another and another.

"Who's the real one?" Warren cried out. "There's only supposed to be one and I found her, all by myself."

He woke up. A low sun was trying to sneak into the forest. The birds started their dawn chorus.

I've lost her, he thought. All by myself.

He crept into the hollow. A bird in the hand was worth two or three in the bush. He snuggled up beside Tina and closed his eyes.

24

The previous morning, after the rescuer had poked his head out of the roof window for the second time, Beedy had flown away. Everything around her had become too chaotic. She flew over the city, south-south-west, coming down in Timberbush.

She was sleeping fifty-five trees away from the others. But the others had no idea. And if you have no idea where someone is, then being close by is no better than being far away.

When she woke up in the early morning, she flew in circles above the forest. She even flew in a circle above the hollow where Warren, Tina, Lottie and the rescuer were sleeping. She didn't spot the hollow. There were so many leaves on the trees, and somewhere beneath them all was the hollow.

Beedy played swap-the-tree all by herself.

She closed her eyes and spun and somersaulted in the air. And when she reached the edge of Timberbush, she saw a glimmering line between the fields. It was a clear running stream that meandered through the countryside. Beedy landed in the middle of the water, which swirled between her toes. She spent hour upon hour in the water, splishing and splashing and getting wet. Her blue jacket cape became wet and heavy. The button wriggled free from its loop. The jacket cape slid from her wings into the water where it was snagged by a stone. Now the stone was wearing a jacket cape.

Beedy didn't notice. She was too busy eating and drinking and playing the whole day long. Not until it began to get dark did she fly away again. She followed the path of the stream from above until she spied a large building beneath her. The building had a lot of small windows that were all open. Beedy explored the roof to see if the chimney would provide a comfortable roosting spot.

She saw a couple of people walking along one side of the building. The other side was deserted. She chose the deserted side and flew a little lower, just beneath the gutter. She looked in the windows. It was deserted inside as well. She saw a little room with a bed and a wardrobe and a chair. There was no one there. Beedy flew to the bed and lay down. The bed was soft, just like the night. She peered outside. The sky continued to darken. A small, lost cloud drifted across the face of the moon.

Occasionally someone walked nearby, down the corridor, but nobody came into the room during the night. Without anyone in the building realizing it, Beedy had found herself another nest. When dawn arrived she flew outside. She played in the stream again. She ate, drank and let the sun shine on her face. At twilight, she returned to her little room where she slept peacefully.

25

Lottie was the first to wake up. She went to find a suitable tree to pee behind. Unfortunately, a beetle was drowned in the flood. By the time she returned, the others were also awake.

"We didn't keep watch," they said, disappointed. "We slept instead."

They felt stiff and numb and they missed being able to have a nice warm shower with pine-scented shampoo.

Slowly they ate their sandwiches and took sparing sips of lemonade.

They were surrounded by a wide world. In such a big place, how would they ever find something as small as Beedy, even when the something small was so very important to them?

They agreed to check every tree in the forest, as high up as they could manage. And also the ground beneath and the sky above. That was more than enough to keep them occupied for the whole day.

They found all sorts of things:

A failed nest

a lost puppy

a strangely shaped stone

an overgrown shoe

an announcement from a newspaper

and a few soft feathers.

"These could be Beedy's," said Tina hopefully.

Further on they found a few more feathers.

They drew an imaginary line. It began at the first lot of feathers and continued on from the second lot to somewhere in the never-ending distance. They followed the line in that direction.

They left the forest as dusk fell.

Soon they crossed the stream where Beedy had been swimming all day.

"At last I can have a wash!" said Tina.

She took off her shoes and pantyhose and stepped carefully onto the smooth stones.

"Ah," she sighed in relief. "Ah…ah…"

Then suddenly, a little further ahead, she saw something blue. At first she imagined it was a handily placed towel. But the blue was exactly the same blue as the jacket cape she had made.

"Beedy," she called out. "There! Beedy's over there!"

The others hurried along the stream bank as Tina stumbled and splashed out of the water.

"Wait, wait for me!" she called out.

She thought they were pulling Beedy out of the water but, as it turned out, it was a stone they were tugging at. A stone wearing a blue jacket cape.

Silently they stared at the stone. Tina took the cape, examined it all over, and clutched it to herself.

Lottie recognized it too. And the rescuer knew right away that the girl in the roof gutter had worn that color.

Warren spoke the words that Tina was thinking.

"It can't be," he said. "This stream is much too shallow to drown in. Beedy pulled her jacket off because it was getting in her way."

"But she couldn't reach the button, could she?" said Tina.

"Buttons come loose by themselves," said Warren. "It can happen quite easily. They have a life of their own when someone's jumping around."

"But what if that someone still needs rescuing?" said the

rescuer. He suggested they follow the stream to see if they could find someone, or something.

It got darker, although there was some light from the moon. The moon looked worried, but then it always did.

The rescuer became anxious that he was about to discover the bones of an eaten-up child. Although birds of prey didn't eat blue jacket capes, they might be able to peel them off their victims, like the skin from an apple.

Tina wanted to believe what Warren had said but other horrible thoughts kept intruding, including one that said a taxidermist had kidnapped Beedy and at this very moment was stuffing her with sawdust, ready to sell to a museum of curiosities.

Lottie wondered whether Beedy might have stepped onto a black paving stone and dropped down into a dreadful cellar and was having her feathers pulled out without any anesthetic.

And Warren thought: birds don't have time for jackets with buttons. They simply don't.

26

A big building with tiny windows stood close to the stream. It had a high front door above which you could read the words Waterview Getovertel.

"*Getovertel*?" said Tina. "What's that?"

"It sounds like a kind of hotel," said the rescuer. "And if it is I'll treat you to a meal and a bed. We need a rest."

An enormous mat lay at the entrance.

It had the word WELCOME written on it.

"We're welcome," said Tina. "That's a good start."

They stepped inside.

A young woman sat behind a desk in the foyer.

"Can we stay here overnight?" asked the rescuer.

"Of course," said the woman. "There's always enough food and plenty of beds. What are you tired of?"

"We're tired of walking and searching and we're hungry and worried."

"You're worried?"

"Yes," said Tina, "but we can't say why."

"Ah," said the woman in a friendly voice. "So your problem is that you find it hard to put things into words."

"We can put our problem into words," said Warren, "as long as it doesn't go any further because it's our secret."

"You can say whatever you like here," said the woman. "Nothing surprises us."

"Well, it's like this," began Warren. "This jacket cape belongs to a sort of girl. But she's really a bird, since she has wings instead of arms.

"My wife badly wants to be able to say goodbye to her. We want to know if someone has seen her. We want to make sure she's okay."

"I understand," said the woman. "Come with me."

She led them through a rose-colored corridor. There were group photos hanging there. The people in them were happy to be together, you could tell.

Then they walked down a yellow corridor. There were drawings hanging there.

In a blue corridor, they were met by a thin man.

"Welcome," he said, just like the mat. "Come into the lounge. Let's have a chat."

The woman was going to return to her desk when the rescuer asked, "Why is this place called a Getovertel instead of a Hotel? Did you have some spare letters?"

"It's because this isn't your usual hotel," said the woman. "It's a hotel where people get better. Everyone here is tired of something, just like you are. We help them get over their tiredness."

"What are they all so tired of?"

"Lots of things," said the woman. "For instance, some can never say what they actually mean. Others are scared they'll never finish anything they start, so they never start anything. Others can't stop thinking about things that they'd be far better off not thinking about at all."

"Such as?"

"Well, such as thinking that flying girls exist, when they don't. Because they're impossible."

27

In the lounge everything was light blue: the tables, the chairs, the walls, the carpet, the lights. Ten people sat amidst all that blue, playing cards or reading the newspaper.

Warren, Tina, Lottie and the rescuer went and sat at one of the blue tables. They were given soup with bread. A lonely meatball swam in each plate. Lottie saved hers for last.

A boy came into the room. He was almost as old as Lottie but he was smaller with shorter hair. He was wearing his pyjamas and had come to say goodnight. He said it to all the people in the lounge. Some answered, "Sleep well." Some said, "Remember now, don't think about spooks and ghosts." Others said nothing at all. It never occurred to them to say goodnight.

The boy came and stood beside Lottie.

"Night," he said.

Lottie had to finish her meatball first. Then she said, "Hi, my name's Lottie, what's yours?"

"Bor," he said, as if he were making a joke.

The thin man came and stood beside them. He put a hand on Bor's shoulder.

"Take the little girl to the room next to yours," he said. "She can sleep there."

Bor scuffed his way to the corridor, followed by Lottie. He was wearing nice pyjamas with a lot of wide-awake words written on them.

"Why are you guys here?" asked Bor.

"To eat and sleep," Lottie answered.

"Yes, but why?" said Bor.

"Just because," said Lottie.

"Do you ever think about things that people say you shouldn't think so much about?" Bor asked.

"I think about so many things," said Lottie. "The things I think are bigger than my head. I can think about a mountain as big as a whole country. Or about the whole world. And I can think about things that are bigger than the world and much further away."

"That's far," said Bor.

"What about you?" asked Lottie.

"I think a lot about ghosts and spirits," said Bor. "On purpose. They say they don't exist. But they actually exist because they don't exist, because they're not made of flesh and blood. They're made of something that isn't there. And I can think about them whenever I want to. But sometimes I think about them when I don't want to. I can imagine a ghost coming out of the plug hole.

"Especially when you use blue toothpaste and spit above the hole. I don't think it works with white toothpaste.

"Or sometimes, if you have to get up to go to the bathroom, one comes out of the toilet bowl just when you're going to sit on it. Then you have to flush quickly.

"Or sometimes there's one under your bed. It starts off small but always turns big really quickly so that while you're lying in bed you get pressed up against the ceiling. And when it gets light, the ghost vanishes and you and the bed come crashing down onto the floor.

"Or there's one that looks so much like a curtain that you think it actually is a curtain waving in the breeze. But it's a ghost that's fighting to get free, while the other half of the curtain calls out, 'Stop that carry-on, I just want to hang here quietly.' And at last the wind blows the window shut and they settle down.

"Or you can hear something ticking in the dark and it turns out to be a knocking spirit trapped inside the central heating pipes. It creeps through the pipes and pushes the knob out, then comes into the room without knocking at all."

"Oh," said Lottie. "I didn't know any of that."

"I don't *know* it either," said Bor, "but it's what I think. Don't tell anyone else because I'm not allowed to think those sorts of thoughts. Promise?"

"Yes," said Lottie. "I like to think I'm a bird because I happen to know one. So that's what I think, and then I am one."

"Good," said Bor. "Now I know what you're thinking. And this is your room.'

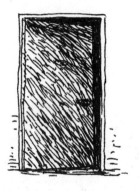

28

In the blue lounge, the thin man had come to sit with Warren, Tina and the rescuer.

"So," he said, "did you enjoy the meal?"

"Yes, we did," said the rescuer. "What's next?"

"Now it's time for you to tell me what thoughts you want to get rid of."

"I have thoughts that I don't want to get rid of at all," said Tina. "Namely that I want a wash and, after that, a nice bed. I'm thinking of those things more than anything else. They're very pleasant thoughts."

"According to your receptionist, we can stay the night," said Warren, "but I'm beginning to think we don't belong here. This is obviously not a typical hotel."

"So that's what you're thinking," said the thin man understandingly.

"Yes," said Warren. "All we want is to get over a busy day. Of course we've all had anxious thoughts in the past but, on the whole, it turned out we didn't need to be anxious. So we don't belong here."

"You're simply in the wrong wing," said the thin man. "Come with me."

Once more they walked down the blue corridor.

"What about Lottie?" Tina asked.

"She's got a lovely room and she'll be well looked after," the thin man said reassuringly.

Now they were going down the yellow corridor.

"Why is everything here yellow?" asked Tina.

"Because this is the Yellow Wing," said the thin man. "I'll explain it to you like this. Here, people are getting over not being able to explain what they're thinking."

"That's a horrible thing," said Tina. "Is it okay if I take a look inside?"

She opened the yellow door of the yellow lounge and put her head round. Her face turned a little pink. She was looking right into the face of another woman.

"I'm only looking," said Tina.

"That's what you say," said the lady angrily. "But it's always anger or anyway how shall I wait a minute."

A man came and stood beside her.

"Obsolete!" he cried. "Without a pergola the pruning is plain and that is quite permissible!"

Tina backed away.

"I didn't understand them," she said, "but they were angry."

"That's why they're so tired," said the thin man. "They mean something but they can't explain themselves."

Tina didn't know what to say in reply. They walked down the length of the yellow corridor and crossed over a green one.

"Who's in there?" she asked.

"In there are the people who think they're failures," said the thin man. "We try to help them get over that. We say over and over again, *Well done*, or, *Carry on with the good work! Great, first rate!* or, *That'll turn out well, you'll see.* Things like that."

"I can relate to that," said the rescuer. "That's what happened to me the last time I had to rescue someone. I'll go and have a look."

He stepped through the door of green lounge. There were

about fifteen people inside. They all wanted to start work on something but were too afraid to begin.

The rescuer squatted down beside a boy sitting on a chair.

"Hello," he said. "Do you feel you're getting over things?"

"No," said the boy. "Everything breaks. Everything. Always."

"That's no good," said the rescuer. "What were you making that broke?"

"I wanted to make something the whole world's waiting for," said the boy, "but nothing ever works."

"That's ambitious, the whole world," said the rescuer. "Wouldn't it be better to begin with something that just one person is waiting for? Tell you what. I'll be that one person. I'll wait until it's finished. Okay?"

"I don't know if it will work," said the boy. "I'm so scared it will break."

"Sometimes broken things are still just as good," said the rescuer. "A broken biscuit tastes as good as a whole one. A broken egg white is still white. And there are some famous works of art that are damaged, or missing a piece or two. In fact, sometimes the most famous part of it is the missing part."

"Is that right?" said the boy.

The rescuer promised to wait and hoped that the boy would manage to make something whole.

Then he went back into the corridor. He looked satisfied. He had the same sort of feeling he got

after he rescued someone and he wanted to hold onto that feeling for as long as he could.

They went into the rose corridor. The thin man opened two bedrooms, one for the rescuer and one for Warren and Tina. They went inside to see what the rooms were like. Because it was dark outside, they couldn't tell if the rooms had nice views. The thin man assured them the views were extra nice, and they had to be satisfied with that. He gave all three of them a pair of slippers.

"You have to wear these," he said. "No one here wears shoes. Shoes are full of dirt from outside."

Feeling somewhat self-conscious, they put the slippers on. The slippers were so floppy and soft they immediately started walking differently in them, like clowns.

"Now I'll take you to the lounge," said the thin man.

"I'd rather have a wash and go to bed," said Tina.

"Drinks are ready for you," said the thin man.

"They know we don't belong here, don't they?" said Warren.

"Yes, they know," said the thin man. "They know that you think that."

He opened the rose-colored door of the rose lounge and pushed them gently inside.

Another group of about fifteen people crowded round them, people who were big and small, fat and thin, old and young. They greeted them like old friends, which they weren't at all.

"Great to see you," they exclaimed. "Now that you're here, everything's going to be even better than it already is."

The people hugged and squeezed them and gave them at least five kisses each. Left cheek, right cheek, left again, right again, and left once more.

They were too frightened to move.

"We're only here to eat and sleep," said the rescuer.

"We don't even belong here," cried Warren.

"Yes," said one of the strangers, as if he understood. "We know what that's like. It's a funny sensation, isn't it? However now you're here, you'll be surprised at how quickly you get over it. We'll make sure you feel like you belong here, one of us, fine people that you are."

And they started to hug them again.

I'm tired, thought Warren.

I want a wash, thought Tina.

The rescuer tried not to think about anything at all.

29

For six days Lottie and Bor acted as if they had known each other for ages. They ate together. They played outside together. If no one was watching, they played ghosts or birds. The people of the Getovertel were happy with their progress.

On the sixth day the thin man said, "Come and sit down so we can have a quiet chat together. What are you two thinking about?"

"I'm thinking about a big mountain," said Lottie.

And Bor said, "I'm thinking about the mountain, too."

The thin man was satisfied with that. He rang Bor's mother and said that Bor was ready to go home because he was a lot better and was no longer obsessed by ghosts and spirits but was thinking about mountains instead.

Bor's mother was very pleased as well. "About mountains," she repeated. "They're lofty thoughts. I'll collect him tomorrow. Thank you for all the trouble you've been to."

During this time, Lottie hadn't given any thought to Beedy. Bor didn't fly away and he was easy to talk to. She'd confided in him about the black paving stones she was afraid of. As it happened, Bor also knew that street very well. He lived not far from it. Lottie hadn't thought about Warren and Tina either. Bor was company enough. They were on vacation together and that was much nicer than searching without having any idea where you were meant to be looking.

And, all this time, Beedy wasn't far away at all. Her bedroom was only four rooms away. Early in the mornings she flew outside to splash in the stream. She ate and drank whatever she liked. She played and flapped and flew in circles above the forest. And as soon as the sunlight stopped tickling her toes, she flew back to her nest in the building.

But at the end of day six, Beedy waited longer than usual to return. She waited until it was completely dark. By accident she flew into the wrong room. Bor's room.

Bor was busy falling asleep but when, by the glow of his night-light, he saw a little ghost fly into the room, he opened his eyes again as wide as he could.

Beedy saw the bed was already occupied. She flew against the ceiling and the walls before coming to rest, motionless, on the chair.

Bor froze as well.

He stared at the dark ghost. It was clear to him that it was small and not at all dangerous. Dangerous ghosts would look quite different in the light of a night-light.

Like this, for example:

Or like this:

The ghost stayed still. Bor heard it breathing. He hadn't
known that ghosts could breath. Breathing made it sound so
alive.

"Hello," he said. "I'm not afraid, you know."

"Eep," said the ghost.

Bor had always believed that a ghost's speech consisted of
oohs and aahs, not eeps.

"I know you don't exist," he said slowly, "but at the same time,
you don't *not* exist and that's the way it is. I can see you're not
not-sitting there. I'm not allowed not to give you something to
drink. That's what we don't not do when someone doesn't not
come to visit, so that's not not allowed, or do you think not not
not or why not?"

By now Beedy had become very tired. She slumped sideways against the back of the chair, put her head between her wings, and fell asleep.

Bor carried on staring at the dark ghost. He was tempted to try and touch it, but he didn't dare. His hand might go right through. And if you didn't feel solid flesh what would you feel? Something that felt like jam or snot or cloud? Slowly he crept from under his blankets and got down on his knees.

As carefully and as quietly as he could, he closed his window.

30

When Bor woke up he saw that the chair was empty. You see, he told himself, ghosts can escape through closed windows. I know all about that.

Right away he went to tell Lottie what had happened. She was the only person in the whole building he could tell. The others would only think that he hadn't got over it yet.

Lottie was sitting on her bed, looking out at the sky.

"Listen to this," said Bor. "I saw a real ghost last night."

"What did it look like?" asked Lottie.

"Pretty small," said Bor, "and harmless."

"Has it gone?"

"Yes. Through the closed window."

Lottie went to Bor's room with him.

"It was sitting there," said Bor, pointing to the chair.

"Did you see it in the dark or the light?"

Bor had seen it in the dark although there had been a little bit of light from the night-light. If it's completely dark you can't see anything of course, even if you want to.

One of the living dead, for example

or a four-sided circle

or a dried-up ocean.

"The ghost's gone," she said. "That's what happens. They disappear at daybreak."

She was about to go, too, when she heard a sound. "Eep."

It came from under Bor's bed. Lottie bent down to look. She saw Beedy lying there, right in the far corner.

"Beedy!" she exclaimed.

She crawled under the bed and pulled Beedy out. She blew the dust off her wings.

"Is it really you?" she said.

"Eep," said Beedy.

Bor watched with wide eyes. This was not a ghost. This was a girl in the shape of a bird. Or a bird in the shape of a girl. Or something in between.

Beedy fluttered up to the ceiling and then let herself flop down on the chair. Where she stayed without moving.

"Where were you?" said Lottie. "We were looking for you. We didn't have a chance to say goodbye."

"Geedbee," said Beedy softly.

"Bye, yes, goodbye. Now I *have* said it. You're not allowed to fly away without saying geedbee. Especially not now. I'm going to find Tina and Warren and the rescuer. They're in the Rose Wing and they were searching for you as well. But they got tired of searching and needed to rest. And they must still be resting because they haven't come to ask me how I'm getting on."

"I weent a seendweech weeth peeneet beettee."

"Yes, you can have one."

Lottie and Bor got dressed. They went to have breakfast. Lottie made a sandwich spread thickly with peanut butter and took it to Beedy. Beedy was under the bed again.

Loose feathers drifted across the floor.

"Now we'll go and find Tina and Warren and the rescuer."

Leaving Beedy behind, they went to the Rose Wing. Carefully they knocked on the door of the lounge. One of the residents of the Getovertel put his head round the door.

"What do you want?" he asked.

"We have to speak to Tina and Warren and the rescuer," said Lottie. "We've got a surprise for them."

Soon the three of them came into the corridor. They were wearing their clown slippers.

"Come with us," said Lottie. "I've got a big surprise for you."

"No, we're not coming," said Warren. "We're staying here."

"We belong here," said Tina.

"Yes," said the rescuer. "It's good here. We're all one happy family.

"Isn't it a pity that you don't belong here? You belong somewhere else instead."

"But we've found Beedy," said Lottie.

At first none of the three said anything. They thought about it instead. It was as if all sorts of things had to be pushed aside from the front of their minds. At last something reappeared that had been hidden in the back of their minds.

"Beedy!"

Tina suddenly found that she had tears in her eyes. "It was the coziness of this place. Everything was so comfy that I stopped thinking about anything else."

"And I completely forgot there might have been an eaten-up girl I should have saved," said the rescuer. "It was easier not to think about that."

"Is Beedy all right?" asked Warren.

"She's fine," said Lottie. "Come and see for yourselves."

First they wanted to say goodbye to the other residents of the rose lounge. That took at least half an hour. They returned with flaming cheeks.

"We'll always be welcome," the rescuer smiled happily. "The doors will always be open for us."

They hurried after Lottie and Bor down the yellow corridor, to the green corridor, and then up the stairs to the top floor.

A cleaner was standing outside Bor's room. She had a cart that carried all her cleaning equipment.

"Don't clean my room!" Bor called out.

"I already have," said the cleaning lady.

"Under the bed as well?"

"Hey, listen you, I don't have to do that every day."

Particles of dust were floating under the bed. The window had been opened wide to let in fresh air. Through his binoculars, Warren saw something flying away in the distance. Something that wasn't in his bird book.

"We're too late," snuffled Tina. "If only we'd remembered her sooner. Now I still haven't said goodbye."

"I have," said Lottie. "And I also made her a peanut butter sandwich. Her favorite."

"She doesn't like a lot of fuss and bother," said Warren. "Everything here must have got too much for her."

They watched the sky for a long time. It was perfect weather for flying.

31

They stayed in Bor's room for a long time. They gathered feathers from under the bed and blew on them.

"I'm going home today," said Bor. "My mother's coming to get me."

"I have to go, too," said Lottie. "My father's coming back. Bor said I can get a ride home with him."

"But I'm still not sure whether there's an eaten-up child lying somewhere," said the rescuer.

"And I still haven't said goodbye to her," said Tina. "For a while there I thought it didn't matter anymore but it does."

"Beedy's flown in a southerly direction," said Warren. "The south is big."

"Should we just go home then?"

"Let's go a little further south, just in case," said Warren. "Until it gets too warm or until we don't feel the need to look anymore, or until we're too tired. Then we'll have done all we could."

Cars drove up outside. They all belonged to people who had come to collect their child or their wife or their husband, or who were simply coming for a visit.

Bor's mother was among them.

She asked if Bor had had a good time, and she wanted to hear the reply, *Yes.*

"Yes," said Bor. He showed Lottie off to his mother as if she was some good news that he'd received. His mother was pleased Lottie was going with them. But first Lottie had to say goodbye. The thin man and the receptionist received only a quick handshake. The goodbyes to Tina, Warren and the rescuer took a lot longer. They promised to visit each other, writing their addresses and telephone numbers on small scraps of paper that could easily have blown away if they hadn't put them deep into their pockets.

When the others drove away, Tina and Warren waved for as long as they possibly could.

Meanwhile the rescuer said, "I'll be back in a jiffy."

He went back inside to the Green Wing. In the lounge he found the boy who had been going to make him something.

The boy looked relieved.

"So you did wait," he said. He reached for a lump of clay. There were a few cracks in it but nothing was broken.

"This is what I made," the boy said. "I've called it *Thoughts*."

"Nice," said the rescuer. "It reminds me of the thoughts I sometimes have."

"So do you think it's worked out okay?"

"Of course it has. Spot on."

"And you don't think the cracks spoil it?"

"Not at all," said the rescuer without hesitation. "They go hand in hand with thoughts."

The boy looked even more relieved.

"I fired the piece," he said, "to make it stronger."

"Excellent," said the rescuer. "Strong, well-baked thoughts. Can I take it with me?"

"Yes," said the boy. "I'm going to make some more. Maybe there'll be other people who want them."

The rescuer shook his hand firmly and went back outside.

"What have you got there?" said Tina.

"Something that someone made specially for me," said the rescuer. "It's called *Thoughts*."

"Oh," said Tina. She did her best to understand the sculpture. But her thoughts looked quite different.

Then they took the road south. They chatted about Lottie and the people in the Rose Wing. Afterwards they talked about Beedy. They walked along paths that were meant to be there, as well as paths that had just formed by themselves. The paths that were meant to be there were ones that someone had imagined first then drawn before they were laid down. The other paths existed only because a lot of people had walked there. If enough people want to walk somewhere, a path forms.

They looked at the sky. They looked under bushes.

Sometimes Tina sniffed. Then she'd say, "Smell that? Everything has its own smell."

They all sniffed. A flower. A small animal. Each other.

"Yes," they said, "everything has its own smell and we don't know how to describe it."

High above, the sun shone down on them.

32

For two days, Tina, Warren and the rescuer trekked south.

They looked up and they looked down. Left and right. And everywhere in between.

They saw a great deal, but they didn't see Beedy.

And the south seemed to have no end.

The first night, they slept in a haystack. Two other people were already sleeping there, but they refused to say "Hi" or "Hello".

All they said was, "We're not really here. We're not really here."

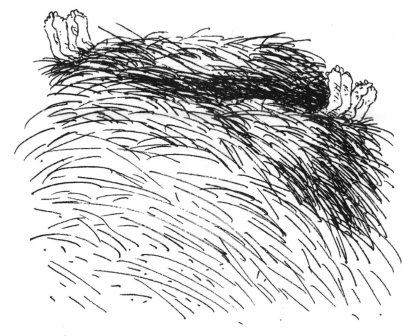

On the evening of the second day, they came upon a pigsty that had been converted into a house.

They walked around the outside of the house and saw a table in the backyard. On the table stood a chair. On the chair stood a stool. On the stool lay a book. On the book stood a young man about twenty years old. He stood upside down, his legs apart and his arms outstretched.

"Look what I can do," he shouted.

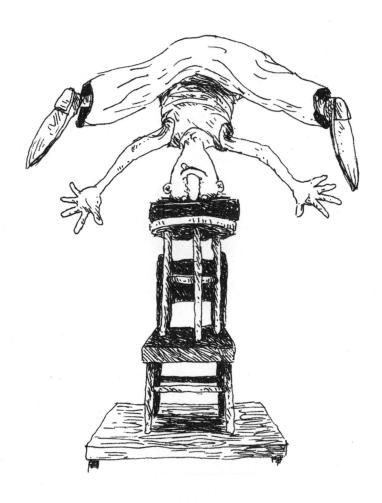

"Be careful, don't fall!" Tina called out to him.

He fell immediately, but luckily he didn't hurt himself.

"That didn't hurt," he said. "I knew it wouldn't. Did you see the risk I took? Did you have a good look? You saw it, didn't you? You were just in time."

The rescuer wanted to help him up, but the young man said he could rescue himself.

Warren asked if they could possibly stay the night. They could. The young man made a big bed of straw in his living room for Warren and Tina. He organized a space for the rescuer in his own bedroom.

Then he got them something to eat. Potatoes and slices of bacon and sour cream to mash into the potatoes.

When the meal was finished, the young man asked if he could show them what else he was bold enough to do. It was much more fun to be daring in front of an audience. Especially when there was someone to exclaim, "Boy, you're brave."

They went outside. The young man climbed up to the top of the sloping roof and balanced there on one leg. He stood on that one leg very elegantly indeed, almost as if he was about to fly away.

"How can you do that?" exclaimed Tina.

"I wasn't brave enough to start with," the young man called down to them. "But I am now because I have a guardian angel protecting me. I saw him last night. It's true, he was only a small guardian angel but that doesn't matter when it comes to protection. As you can see."

He balanced on his other leg.

"I couldn't sleep last night," the young man said. "I was tossing and turning. Suddenly I saw the angel, sitting on the windowsill. I saw the wings. I saw my own guardian angel."

"But that wasn't..." began Tina. Warren shushed her, his hand in front of her mouth.

"Shush," he said. "Don't say anything. He's balancing on the roof on one leg."

"Yes, of course," Tina whispered. "He must have seen Beedy. But we won't say anything because then he might fall down."

33

They spent the evening in the young man's living room. The young man shared soda and warm milk and lots of stories. He told them all the daring things he still wanted to do. Such as:

Walking through the jungle in the middle of the night without being scared either of the dark or the jungle.

Tightrope walking high above

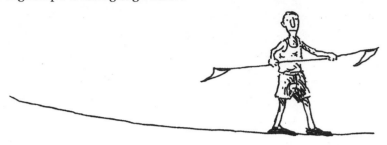

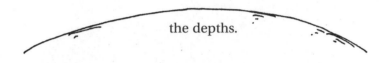

the depths.

Cleaning the teeth of a tiger.

"But, then, I'd need an audience," he said.

"Do you live here all alone?" asked Tina.

"I didn't to start with," said the young man. "I used to live with twenty pigs but they got a rare disease and had to be put down. My job died with them and I was too scared to try anything new. I was scared of catching a rare disease. But now I'm not scared of anything."

"You'd make a good rescuer," said the rescuer. "Rescuers have to be risk-takers. Would you like to become one? I could help you, since I'm a rescuer myself."

"See!" exclaimed the young man. "Everything's working out well because of my guardian angel. He sent you. I'd love to become a rescuer. I've often seen them on television. It's exciting, with lots of blood. Will I get cups and medals and things like that? I hope there's lots of trouble because then I'll have lots to do."

It was late when they went to sleep. Warren and Tina crawled into their bed of straw in the living room while the rescuer crept into his, next to the bed of the young man.

The rescuer felt uncomfortable. The straw prickled his back and bottom. He missed his old father and mother. He knew his mother would be looking out for him each day, peering through the red flowers, hoping he was on the way home. He thought about all the emergencies that were happening while he wasn't there and how much he was missing his rescuing job. He wanted to go home.

Then suddenly he saw Beedy fly through the open window and settle on the windowsill. With the light of the full moon behind her, she really did look like an angel. The rescuer lay there watching. He kept absolutely still. The angel was close by, yet unreachable. Now he was certain. There was no eaten-up girl and there were still wonders left in the world.

Beedy perched on the windowsill for a while longer. But it was too crowded and stifling indoors. She flew away again. She crept underneath a table outside, the same table on which the chair was standing. It was the chair on which the stool stood. It was the stool on which the book rested. It was a book about landscapes.

The rescuer fell asleep feeling enormously happy. He dreamed that he, too, had wings. He flew above the street where he lived. His father and mother were watching from the front step. They called out to him, "Dinner's ready at six. Are you coming back down then? It's your favorite meal!" And they called out the name of his favorite meal, but he couldn't understand the words. All he heard was *matoemebals* and *fresbred.* And he had no idea how absolutely marvelous that could taste.

34

Over breakfast, the rescuer described how he'd seen "you-know-who" during the night, the guardian angel, the one with a jacket cape and feathers, and how he had seen her, with his own eyes, in the middle of the night. He said that he was now completely at peace with himself and no longer scared of birds of prey. And he said that he wanted to go home. If the young man wanted to go with him he would be most welcome. Together they'd go to the rescue services where he would ask if the young man could become a trainee rescuer. He was sure it would be possible, if he asked, because he was the best rescuer in the whole city and beyond.

The young man went at once and got his toothbrush. The four of them ambled to the bus stop, half an hour away. They had to wait a long time for a bus. To make the time pass more quickly, Warren told them about the lives of the dotterel and the linnet. The rescuer told the young man what sort of unexpected things you had to watch out for as a rescuer. There were a great many such things. The young man couldn't remember them all at once.

After that, Tina and Warren said their goodbyes in advance. There is never enough time to do that when the bus comes. The rescuer didn't know whether to kiss Tina once, twice or three times. The third kiss hung in the air between them. Perhaps the sky is full of kisses, invisible, but there nonetheless. They promised to visit each other and to send cards with *How goes it with you? It's going well with me* written on them.

When the bus finally arrived they said, "We've already said our goodbyes." But they did it again anyway, otherwise it seemed too sudden an end.

The rescuer and the young man got on the bus and sat in the the back. The four of them could see each other for quite a while until the bus turned a bend and swallowed them up.

Warren and Tina were left alone together, somewhere between the city and the south.

"Oh, Warren," said Tina.

"Oh, Tina," said Warren.

"Why did all the others see Beedy and we didn't? I did so much for her."

"She might not be far away," said Warren. "She's always stayed in the area. As it turned out she hadn't flown very far south at all. So let's keep our hope alive, for another day at least, that we'll see her again. And after that, let's keep on thinking that things happened as they were supposed to happen."

They took a sandy path, not noticing if it led north, east, south or west.

The dusty sand felt soft. Their shoes suddenly looked old.

Tina asked herself what the word was for the sound her shoes made in the sand. Walking on gravel sounded crunchy. This sounded more like a sigh. There were so many things that had no words to describe them. You could invent a word but unless everybody knew it, it was useless. Except for some words that only a handful of people had to know in order to be able to use them. Warren knew exactly what she meant when she said *heneth* or *yosh*. He knew that.

Suddenly they heard a gunshot.

Only now did they see the line of hunters in the distance. They were walking up a rise in a field. They were almost at the top.

"Don't shoot!" Tina called out, frightened.

But the hunters didn't hear her. Even if they had, they wouldn't have taken any notice. Because if they didn't shoot there wouldn't be any point being there. They might as well have stayed at home.

Tina and Warren ran towards the hunters. They didn't stop to think that, from a distance, they might look like deer or rabbits or some other tasty four-legged target.

"Stop that right now," Tina yelled. "Stop it, will you! Don't you know how dangerous that is?"

Breathless, she and Warren came to a halt. For a time they heard only the wind. Then came another shot, but from further away.

The hunters had disappeared behind the hill.

"We've chased them off," said Warren proudly.

They left the field, their shoes now heavy with clay. It made them walk differently.

Back on the asphalt their shoes made a new sound. If there was a word for it, it would have sounded like the word *slurp*, said breathing in. That word was already used to mean something else, but never mind. It didn't matter. There were enough words that had more than one meaning. And when you heard them, you didn't get them mixed up.

They tried to clean their shoes without getting their hands dirty. They dirtied a clump of moss instead. They picked up a stick from under a tree to use as a scraper.

And then they saw something lying there, half under a bush. It looked like a bird of prey but it wasn't anything listed in Warren's bird book. Something with legs. And with two wings, where people had arms.

"Beedy!" cried Tina.

"Eep," peeped Beedy.

35

A shot of lead had flown straight through the lowest part of Beedy's left wing. In one side and out the other (just where the soft feathers were).

Lots of loose feathers lay on the ground.

Warren lifted Beedy up and, once again, nestled her in his arms. Tina gathered up the loose feathers. Maybe she could stick them back where they belonged, with super-glue perhaps.

"We're going home," said Warren. "Right now."

They took the first bus that came along. When the bus got to a railway station, they got off and boarded a train.

Beedy weighed next to nothing. She seemed unconscious. On the journey home everything was moving, except Beedy.

They didn't arrive home until the end of the day.

It took another two days for Beedy to wake up, and it took a lot longer before she could use her wing again.

Tina decided not to super-glue the feathers back on. She made a small, new wing with them. She laid it on the table, just for looking at.

Slowly but surely, Beedy's left wing healed. She began to flap it a little. Then she made small, fluttering jumps. Soon she was flying up to perch on the china cabinet.

"I think she's getting ready to fly away again," said Warren. "South. I think she wants to head south. We won't stop her."

"But isn't it nice and warm inside?" said Tina.

"Yes," said Warren, "but some birds and other animals just have that instinct. They feel a pull to the south."

Tina understood. You couldn't keep birds forever, except in your thoughts.

"Then we'll have to say goodbye in plenty of time," she said. "I don't want her up and leaving before I've got used to the idea. Although I'm already used to it."

That same afternoon, Warren went into town. He bought a golden ring that would easily fit Beedy's big toe. *Bon voyage* was engraved inside.

Tina spent the whole afternoon making a special farewell dinner. Alphabet noodle soup. Then they could eat "goodbye" and "until we meet again".

And she made a pancake stack. And she prepared lightly-cooked spiders on a bed of grain and her own recipe of browned beetle.

She set the table extra nicely. She decorated Beedy's eating apparatus with twigs from the garden.

And she opened a bottle of champagne. They'd kept the bottle a long time, ready for a special occasion. A few times, when it felt like a special occasion, they'd asked each other, "Is it a special occasion?"

But each time they'd decided it wasn't quite special enough. But now it was.

Between them they finished the bottle and got a bit happy and giggly. They hopped around the room behind Beedy and almost felt as if they were defying gravity. A small, fluttering amount. Such a miniscule amount that you couldn't see it, only feel it.

Beedy left the morning after the little celebration. Through the open window into the wide sky. Heading south.

Tina and Warren looked under the table, on the china cabinet, under the bed.

"She's gone," said Warren.

"To the south," said Tina.

They wanted to go south too, but they belonged in the north. Sometimes the north could be warm enough, if it wasn't cold.

"Perhaps she'll come back one day," said Tina.

Warren went outside and gazed at the sky above the countryside.

For a second he thought he could still see Beedy.

But it was just a fleck on his binoculars.

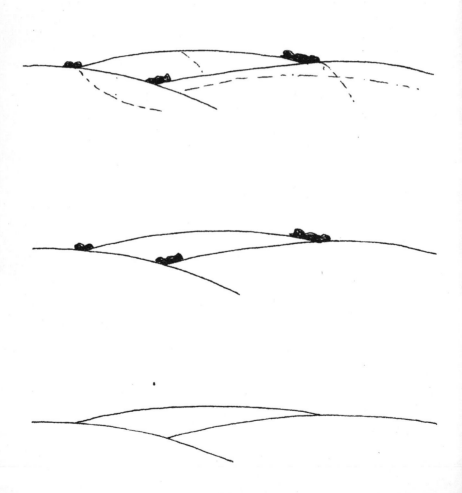

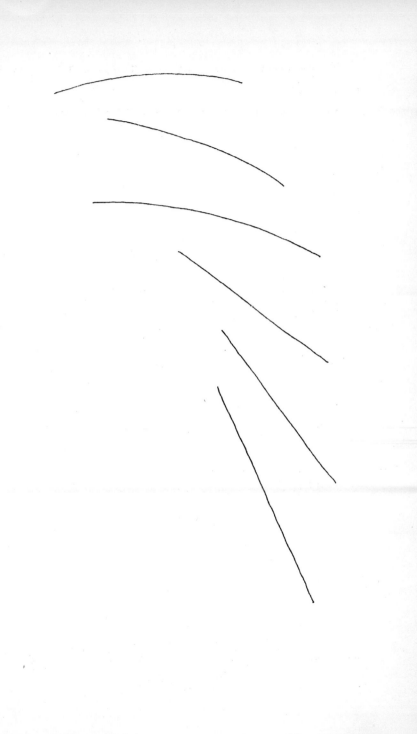